PUFFIN BOOKS

The Lost War Dog

Praise for Megan Rix from Young Readers:

"*The Bomber Dog* is heart-warming and tear-drawing . . .
It's a great book to read on a rainy day to bring all sorts of
emotions like joy and sadness." Fergus Wynne

"I loved this book . . . I give this book 1000/1000 and
would recommend it for 7+ and people who like a bit of
animal drama." Emma Payne

"This book is a great book to read and learn about
the war." Owen Chapman

"I like this book because it is exciting, adventurous and funny.
I couldn't stop reading it because it was so gripping."
The Guardian's Children User Reviews

"I enjoyed it so much that I read it as I walked to school,
between lessons and at every other opportunity."
The Guardian's Children User Reviews

D0237647

popular author of animal adventure books set in the modern day and key periods of history. An animal advocate and dog friend, Megan draws inspiration from her own adorable dogs Traffy, Bella, Freya and Ellie.

Follow Megan Rix on Twitter

@megan_rix

#LostWarDog

Books by Megan Rix

THE GREAT FIRE DOGS

THE BOMBER DOG

THE GREAT ESCAPE

THE VICTORY DOGS

A SOLDIER'S FRIEND

THE RUNAWAYS

ECHO COME HOME

THE HERO PUP

THE PAW HOUSE

For younger readers

ROSA AND THE DARING DOG

WINSTON AND THE MARMALADE CAT

EMMELINE AND THE PLUCKY PUP

FLORENCE AND THE MISCHIEVOUS KITTEN

The Lost War Dog

megan rix

PUFFIN

PUFFIN BOOKS

UK | USA | Canada | Ireland | Australia
India | New Zealand | South Africa

Puffin Books is part of the Penguin Random House group of companies
whose addresses can be found at global.penguinrandomhouse.com.

www.penguin.co.uk
www.puffin.co.uk
www.ladybird.co.uk

Set in 13/16 pt Baskerville MT
Typeset by Jouve (UK), Milton Keynes
Printed and bound in Great Britain by Clays Ltd, Elcograf S.p.A.

A CIP catalogue record for this book is available from the British Library

ISBN: 978-0-241-45555-5

All correspondence to:
Puffin Books
Penguin Random House Children's
One Embassy Gardens, 8 Viaduct Gardens
London SW11 7BW

MIX
Paper from
responsible sources
FSC
www.fsc.org
FSC® C018179

Penguin Random House is committed to a
sustainable future for our business, our readers
and our planet. This book is made from Forest
Stewardship Council® certified paper.

'Who finds a faithful friend finds a treasure'
Jewish proverb

Chapter 1

In the quiet early hours of the morning, a small black-and-tan dachshund, wearing a woven collar of red and gold, made her nightly patrol. She froze as an icy draught caught hold of the threadbare curtains and forced them into a ghostly dance. Outside the window she watched as long red, black and white flags flapped in the moonlight.

The curtains stilled and the dachshund slipped off the bed and padded out through the half-open door. In the living room a man slept on the worn sofa, snoring softly, his legs hanging over the end. His hands clasped a thin blanket, his feet were still in his socks, and his black beard, streaked with grey, was spread over the cushion he was using for a pillow.

In the kitchen, the few dropped crumbs from supper were gone. The dachshund's black nose sniffed at the spot under the stove where, just a few moments before, a little mouse's whiskers had been poking out.

She headed out of the kitchen and in through another door, where two elderly people lay fast asleep in the double bed that almost filled the small room. The old woman made a soft whistling sound as she slept. The old man snored and slapped his lips together every now and again. On the small bedside table there was a framed medal from the 1914 War and a photo of a young woman holding a baby.

The dog sat and watched the old people for a while. Her intelligent, inquisitive eyes were able to see far more in the dark than human eyes could. At last, satisfied all was well, she trotted back to where she had come from – the box bedroom at the back of the flat, where two more people slept soundly in a pair of beds that were squashed inside.

The dachshund's short legs jumped easily on to the nearest bed. She curled up, but didn't go back to sleep. The little dog listened and waited, waited for another day to begin.

When thirteen-year-old Tilly Abrams awoke hours later, the first thing she saw was her little dog lying in her usual place at the bottom of the bed.

'Morning, Wuffly!' she smiled, before pushing back her tangled long black hair and rubbing at her sleepy eyes.

Wuffly came racing up the bed for a morning cuddle, her tail wagging happily. Tilly stroked the dachshund's soft furry head.

'Did you have a good sleep?' she asked.

Wuffly rolled over on to her back with her legs in the air so Tilly could give her a tummy rub.

'That dog should be sleeping on the floor, not your bed,' said a muffled voice from underneath the blankets of the other narrow bed. The room was so small the two beds were almost touching. 'Or outside being a guard dog – earning its keep.'

Tilly chuckled. 'Wuffly's a bit small to be a guard dog, Aunt Hedy! I can't imagine who she'd be able to scare away.'

Wuffly rolled over again and gave Tilly's hand a lick to ask for more belly rubs.

'Plus, it's too cold for Wuffly to be outside all night,' Tilly added as she stroked the dog's smooth fur. It had been threatening to snow in Hamburg all week.

'Just better not go on my bed,' said Aunt Hedy. 'I don't want fleas.'

'Never,' said Tilly with a smile.

She was absolutely sure Wuffly never ventured on to her aunt's bed – at least not when Aunt Hedy was looking!

'Unhygienic,' came Aunt Hedy's sleepy reply as she turned over on to her stomach.

'Don't take any notice. She's always a bit grouchy in the morning,' Tilly whispered to Wuffly. She hopped out of bed and the little dog jumped down after her. Aunt Hedy could be a bit of a grouch in the mornings . . . afternoons *and* evenings too. Aunt Hedy was so different from how Tilly's mum had been. It was strange how unalike two sisters could be.

'Such a *lobbus*,' Aunt Hedy grumbled as she picked up Tilly's pillow and threw it after her.

Tilly grinned at her aunt's use of the Yiddish word for 'cheeky', grabbed the pillow that had landed on the floor and threw it back at her.

'*Lobbus* yourself!'

Tilly and Wuffly ran out of the flat and along the hallway to the third-floor communal toilet. It was shared by everyone who lived on the third floor.

At Tilly's old house, not far from where her best friend Gretchen still lived, the family had had their own toilet. Tilly sighed. Her mum had still been alive then too. Everything had been better.

In March, not long after her mum's funeral, the *Gestapo* (Germany's secret police) had forced them to move out of their old house. The family had still been reeling from the loss of her mum when they'd rented this flat in Grindel, the Jewish quarter of Hamburg.

Tilly really missed their old house, her old room, and not being able to play with Wuffly outside in the garden. But most of all she missed her mum.

The doctors and nurses at the Jewish hospital had tried their best to treat Mum's pneumonia – Tilly knew they'd done everything they could for her, but it wasn't enough. That was when Opa and Oma came to live with them permanently. Then a few months ago, Aunt Hedy had joined them.

'I know you miss Mum too,' Tilly said to Wuffly as they reached the end of the hallway to the communal toilet. They all missed her, even though they didn't always say so.

Tilly pulled open the wooden door and held her breath. She tried to use the toilet in the flats as little as possible, partly because it could get very smelly with over twenty people having to use it. But worse, Tilly hated the fact that there was a big spider living somewhere inside. She could never be sure where it was lurking, or when it would come scuttling towards her.

'You come in with me,' she told Wuffly.

Maybe Wuffly would gobble the spider up for breakfast. She smiled at the thought, and then abruptly stopped as she imagined the creature going after Wuffly instead. She certainly didn't like to think of a creepy-crawly running around inside Wuffly's tummy.

Tilly looked up at the ceiling. There it was, hiding in the corner.

'You just stay there,' she told it sternly. The spider didn't move.

A moment later there was a banging on the door.

'Have you got a dog in there? Dogs aren't allowed!' a voice shouted.

'One minute,' Tilly called back.

Wuffly sat on the floor of the toilet and looked at Tilly with one ear up and one ear down.

Tilly opened the door to find Mrs Jacobs from number 31 standing outside with her hands on her hips.

'I should report you to the landlord,' Mrs Jacobs said.

'I'm sorry. I was frightened of the big spider.'

'Huh!' said Mrs Jacobs. 'A Jewish girl frightened of a little spider –'

'It's not little –' Tilly interrupted.

But Mrs Jacobs pushed past Tilly to go into the toilet herself. 'There's a lot worse things for you to be scared of in Hamburg. Much worse, believe me!'

Chapter 2

'Breakfast's ready, Mathilde,' her grandmother called out, just as she and Wuffly came back into the flat.

'Coming, Oma!' Tilly first washed her hands in the china bowl filled with hot water in her bedroom, and then came hurrying into the small kitchen with Wuffly right behind her.

Her father, aunt and grandfather were already eating, although her grandfather was sitting in his armchair while the others sat round the small rickety table because there wasn't enough space for everyone. It didn't matter as her grandfather loved the armchair and sat in it from the moment he woke up until he went to bed.

'Morning, Opa,' Tilly signed to the old man.

'Morning,' his hands waved back.

'There was no bread left by the time Jewish people were allowed to buy it yesterday,' Aunt Hedy said with a sigh as Oma put a bowl of watery porridge down on the table in front of Tilly.

'Porridge is good,' Tilly's dad said. 'It's filling.'

Aunt Hedy walked out of the kitchen to do her hair. Every day she went to the Jewish community centre that had opened in January.

Tilly nodded as she took a mouthful. It *was* filling, although it would have been nice with a bit of sugar or honey on it, and even better made with milk instead of water.

Her father was wearing the one good suit he had left. All his other suits, as well as anything any of them could spare, had been sold to bring in more money for food and other expenses, like Wuffly's dog licence. Every dog in Hamburg was issued with an official number and given a little disc with the number on it. Wuffly had to wear it on her collar along with her name tag. But at least Tilly's father still had a job. When she was at elementary school he used to work as a station master at the train station. But that was before the railway company decided to fire Jewish people, and those who were married to Jewish people. Now her dad worked in a men's clothes shop run by Mr Rubenstein, an old Jewish school friend. It didn't pay as well as his other job, and it was a step down to be a junior assistant, but at least it paid something. It meant they didn't have to ask the Jewish community centre for help to buy food like lots of other people now did.

Aunt Hedy had come to live with them because she had lost her job as a secretary. She hadn't yet been able to find other employment, although she was looking.

When Aunt Hedy had first moved in, she'd said she had become a Zionist and wanted to leave Germany and go to Palestine as soon as she could. Aunt Hedy was now taking Hebrew lessons and had recently graduated from the Jewish Professional School for Seamstresses. Tilly thought back to that time. 'Once we have a homeland of our own, Jewish people will be safe,' she had told Tilly.

The memory caused Tilly to ask, 'Why does Herr Hitler hate us so much?' It seemed as if he wanted to make life impossible for Jewish people. 'I hate him!'

'Sssh!' cried Oma. 'Do you want to bring the *Gestapo* down on us?'

'Sorry,' Tilly whispered. 'But it's so unfair.'

Her father sighed and shook his head. 'Who knows what goes on in the mind of a dictator,' he said softly. 'But it's not just *us* he hates. He hates gypsies and disabled people . . .'

'But Jews most of all,' Tilly said miserably.

'You'd think his words were diamonds the way most German people hang on every one of them,' hissed Oma.

'And anyone who doesn't believe his words are diamonds had better pretend that they do,' Aunt Hedy warned them all as she came back in. 'There are spies everywhere – even the walls have ears; so watch what you say unless you want to end up like poor Mister Kowalski. Polish Jews have it even worse than German Jews.'

'What happened to Mister Kowalski?' Tilly asked.

'Well, he didn't want to return to Poland with the other seventeen thousand Polish Jews ten days ago during the –'

'*Polenaktion?*' said Tilly. Everyone had heard about it. People had been ripped from their lives and forced to leave Germany at a moment's notice.

Aunt Hedy nodded. 'Yes, and who can blame him for not wanting to be deported to Poland? He'd been living in Hamburg for over thirty years – ever since he was a baby. The poor man couldn't even speak Polish!'

'It's terrible. I don't condone it, but I wasn't surprised when I read about the Polish Jewish teenager Herschel Grynszpan – who was actually born in Germany – taking matters into his own hands . . .' Mr Abrams said.

'What did he do?' Tilly asked her father.

Usually her family tried not to talk about politics in front of her, but she thought she was old enough to hear. They couldn't protect her forever!

'He shot a Nazi diplomat called Ernst vom Rath,' Aunt Hedy replied. Her dad gave Aunt Hedy a warning look.

'But why?' Tilly asked, her brown eyes wide.

Aunt Hedy looked at Tilly's dad and then said quickly, 'Because his sister managed to send him a postcard from the border of Poland, begging him for help.'

'Hedy . . .' Tilly's dad said, but Aunt Hedy took no notice.

'Thousands of Polish Jews, including Herschel's family, were stranded and barely surviving on handouts from the Red Cross. The lucky ones were living in limbo in concentration camps. Others were forced to live in pigsties and stables in freezing conditions.'

Tilly's dad stood up. 'And Ernst vom Rath, the Nazi who was shot, might die from his injuries, and for what? Nothing, that's what,' he said. 'Now enough of this. Eat your porridge before it gets cold.'

'But what about Mister Kowalski?' Tilly asked.

'No one knows for sure,' Aunt Hedy told her. 'Some say he's been put in a concentration camp for protesting. Others, well . . .' She looked over at Tilly's dad. 'One thing's for sure.'

'What?'

'It won't be good.'

With her tongue hanging out, Wuffly sniffed at the porridge Tilly was spooning into her mouth.

At that moment there was a loud thumping on the door and they all jumped up, apart from Opa, who couldn't hear the knocking.

Aunt Hedy cried out, making Oma drop her spoon with a clatter. Wuffly gave a big *woof*.

'The *Gestapo*!'

Chapter 3

'You know it's *not* the *Gestapo*,' Tilly said, recognizing the familiar rhythm of three quick knocks followed by two slow ones. Her aunt visibly relaxed, and headed out of the kitchen.

Oma looked over at Tilly and shook her head. She recognized the rhythm too. 'She shouldn't keep coming here – she doesn't *belong*,' Oma said.

Despite this, Tilly ran to the door to let her friend in, with Wuffly right behind her.

'Only Jews can live in Grindel,' Oma continued. 'Not *goys*. She'll get in trouble – and so will we!'

'Morning!' said the girl standing in the doorway. She was tall and blonde, with blue eyes and freckles over the bridge of her nose. She grinned at Tilly. Tilly grinned back at her.

'Gretchen – come in,' Tilly said, moving to the side to let her friend in.

Opa signed 'Good morning' to Gretchen and Gretchen signed 'Good morning' in return. She didn't know as many signs as Tilly did, but she knew some and liked using them.

'My dad's on earlies,' she told everyone. Gretchen's father was a train driver at the station where Tilly's dad used to work. 'And Mum's also at the station. She's waiting for Fritz to come home from the Hitler Youth Camp. I thought we could walk to school together, Tilly.' She pulled two parcels wrapped in brown paper from her school bag. 'I made us lunch.'

'Thanks!' Tilly said gratefully as Wuffly sniffed at the delicious-smelling paper.

Gretchen lived more than an hour's walk away, and it was another half an hour from Tilly's flat to the school. Today Gretchen had come on her bicycle.

Tilly put the strawberry jam sandwiches in her school bag and hitched it on to her shoulder.

'Morning, Gretchen,' Aunt Hedy said, coming out of the box bedroom with her hair now in a low bun. She gave Tilly's unruly hair a quick brush and put it in a plait for her.

'This hair is getting so long you could sit on it,' she said.

'I can already, just about,' Tilly told her.

'Mmm, porridge,' said Gretchen as she looked at the steam coming from the bowls.

Oma filled another bowl and handed it to Gretchen, who quickly tucked in. 'Your porridge is the best, Oma – there's no lumps at all!' she said between mouthfuls.

Wuffly gave a small whine; she hadn't had her breakfast yet.

'We'd better get going,' Tilly said when Gretchen had finished her porridge. 'I can't eat all of mine, Oma. Wuffly can have this last bit!'

Oma nodded as she took Tilly's bowl and scraped the leftover porridge into Wuffly's bowl. The little dog wagged her tail as she watched.

Once they were on the street, Tilly looked back at their third-floor apartment window and waved to Wuffly, who was exactly where Tilly had expected her to be. The dachshund pressed her paw to the glass.

'See you soon, Wuffly,' Gretchen called out loudly.

Tilly waved again as Gretchen took her bicycle from the rack. She knew that the little dog was barking now by the way she was jumping about and opening and closing her mouth. Aunt Hedy wouldn't be pleased about the noise!

Gretchen's was the only bicycle in the rack because Jewish people weren't allowed to have bicycles any more. Tilly really missed having a bike.

Gretchen held the handlebars and pushed her bicycle along beside her friend. The two of them walked past the huge synagogue with its beautiful stained-glass windows on Bornplatz, and then past the clothes shop where Tilly's dad worked. There were a couple of men who usually stood outside the shop all day, holding up placards that read DON'T BUY FROM JEWS, but Tilly was relieved that they hadn't arrived yet. She hated seeing them. A few months ago the word *Jude*, which meant 'Jew', had been painted on the shopfront window in big thick red letters, using hard-to-remove oil paint.

Mr Rubenstein and her dad had tried to scrub it off, but they got into even more trouble for doing so. Not only were they fined by the government, but Hitler's SA Storm Troopers (or Brownshirts, as everyone called them because of their brown uniform) had repainted JUDE in even bigger letters, and added a six-pointed Star of David alongside it with a picture of a little hanging man. Other shopfront windows along the street had JUDE, or JUDEN, painted on them too. Tilly looked at the ground. Usually she went the long way to school so she could avoid this street, but today Gretchen was with her.

Fortunately Gretchen loved talking and didn't notice her discomfort. She told Tilly how her parents were hoping her older brother Fritz might be selected for one of the *Führer*'s prestigious boarding schools.

'That'll be nice,' Tilly said flatly.

All the boys in her school were in the Hitler Youth, which meant they wore a brown uniform and a swastika flag armband on their left arm. They marched down the streets holding flags, played sports and went camping.

All the girls in Tilly's class were in the girls' part of the Hitler Youth. They wore a blue skirt and a white blouse with a silver and black triangle badge on it, and a black neckerchief fastened with a brown leather knot. Tilly hadn't been allowed to join because she was Jewish. The teacher had given out forms in the class for the children to take home, but when Tilly asked for one the teacher had ignored her.

All Aryan Germans had to belong to the organization by law. At the moment Gretchen was in the JM – the Young Girls' League – but when she was fourteen, she'd be in the BDM, the League of German Girls.

'What do you do at the meetings?' Tilly had asked when Gretchen first joined. All she knew was that the meetings happened twice a week.

'Practise our *Heil Hitler* salutes and march about,' Gretchen told her. 'Sometimes we sing patriotic songs. The boys get to use weapons and run assault courses; the girls do gymnastics.'

Tilly knew Gretchen liked gymnastics. She liked all kinds of sports and was really good at *bosseln*, a game where you had to throw a wooden ball as far as you could. Professionals could throw it over 100 metres! Gretchen couldn't throw it that far, but she was the best at it in their school.

In the summer, the German Young Girls' League had gone camping, which Tilly thought Gretchen would have liked very much, but she'd said it was boring without Tilly.

'*And* we all got bitten by midges.'

She had let Tilly look at the Hitler Youth monthly magazine, *Will and Power*. But it contained a whole page about Jews being bad and stupid, so Tilly had given it back to her quickly. She wondered if Gretchen had even read the magazine.

'It's not fair. The older boys are given a knife with the *Blood and Honour* motto engraved on it. Girls should be given one too,' Gretchen complained.

As they walked up the street to school, Gretchen turned to Tilly with a smile. 'My mum and dad said there's going to be a surprise for Jewish people very soon,' she said.

'What is it?' Tilly asked doubtfully. Recently there'd been a lot of not-very-nice surprises for Jewish people, like not being able to own a private garden, being kicked out of work, not having enough food, no bicycles . . . rules, rules and more unfair rules everywhere.

'I don't know,' Gretchen said, 'but Mum and Dad sounded excited, like it was a really good thing for a change. They said they were especially glad Fritz would be back in time for it.'

'I wonder what it could be,' Tilly said nervously.

'Maybe Jewish children are going to be allowed to play in the parks again or go swimming at the pools,' Gretchen said hopefully.

'Maybe,' smiled Tilly as they went in through the school gates. It had been more than two years since she'd been allowed to do either. But she could still hope.

Wuffly had stayed at the window, looking out, long after Tilly had disappeared.

Around her, the other members of the family continued with their day. Tilly's father left for work and Opa went with him as far as the synagogue. He couldn't hear the prayers any more, but he liked to sit on the benches and enjoy the peacefulness of the place, looking up at the beautiful painted ceiling.

Later, Oma started preparing meatloaf for supper, although there was barely enough meat in it to feed a mouse (and the kitchen mouse was full from the porridge that had fallen on the floor when Oma had dropped her spoon that morning).

Wuffly jumped off the windowsill and headed to the front door as Aunt Hedy put a scarf round her hair and pulled on her coat.

'I'm off to my Hebrew class,' she called out to Oma.

'Have fun, Hedwig,' Oma replied.

As soon as Wuffly saw the front door open a crack, she raced past Hedy and down the stairs.

'No! Wuffly, Wuffly, come back!' Aunt Hedy's voice called after her, but the little dog didn't even pause. Hedy's shoes clattered down the stairs, but she had no chance of catching Wuffly when she was in a determined mood.

Wuffly panted as she ran along the now busy street, past the men holding the DON'T SHOP HERE signs outside the Jewish shops, narrowly avoiding the hands of pedestrians and brown-shirted boys who tried to grab her.

At last she turned the corner into the street that led to Tilly's school.

Chapter 4

'Tilly Toadstool! Tilly Toadstool!' A group of children circled Tilly, pointing at her.

'Stop it! Stop it!' Tilly yelled, putting her hands over her ears.

Gretchen put her hands on her hips. 'What's going on?'

'It's in this book,' one of the children told her, holding up a picture of what looked like a mushroom with an old man's face in it. 'It shows you how to tell if someone's a Jew.'

'In the same way that you can't always spot if a toadstool or mushroom is poisonous, you can't always know when someone's a Jew just by looking at them!' said someone else. 'This book tells you what to look out for.'

'You're a poisonous mushroom, Mathilde.'

'Don't come near me! *I* don't want to get poisoned.'

'What a load of old rubbish!' Gretchen shouted. 'You lot have smaller *brains* than a mushroom!'

One of the boys clenched his fists, but so did Gretchen. 'Want to fight about it?'

Tilly wasn't as tall or strong as Gretchen, who was the tallest girl in their class. But she felt so angry about all the times she'd been picked on or left out, forbidden to do this, forbidden to do that – and never allowed to make a fuss or cause a scene.

'Tilly Toadstool!' a girl shouted in her face.

With that, a cry of pure fury came from Tilly as she launched herself at the taunting girl, and then the one next to her, punching and kicking and biting like a thing possessed. There were far more children than Tilly could possibly fight, but in the next moment Gretchen was fighting right alongside her.

Now none of the children were calling her names. Blouses and shirts were torn, hair pulled, faces scratched.

Tilly's long plait was yanked and came undone. She was pushed to the hard muddy ground and kicked, but she managed to grab the boy's leg and pull him down as well. She scrambled up to see Gretchen holding off three punching children at the same time.

'Stop this at once!' the headmaster roared, running over with Tilly's teacher to pull the fighting children apart.

'She started it,' one of the boys said, pointing at Tilly.

'I did not!' Tilly shouted, lunging at the boy. '*You* did with that stupid book.'

The headmaster grabbed her by the arm and held on to it firmly.

'I might have known it would be your fault,' he said; his breath had the sour smell of coffee. 'This sort of behaviour just proves what the *Führer* has long suspected. That *Juden* are inferior.'

Tilly's mouth fell open. 'We're not!' she said, pulling her arm away and rubbing where he'd held it far too tightly. People were always saying things like that. How could they possibly believe it?

'It's not her fault,' one girl said, bringing Tilly some relief, until she added, '*Juden* have small heads, which means only tiny brains can fit inside it.'

Tilly remembered Gunther, a boy in the year below, telling her his teacher had measured his head in front of the whole class, and then lied and said it was smaller than everyone else's. After that Gunther's parents sent him to a Jewish school instead.

Now Tilly was the only Jewish student left at her school.

'That's not true!' Tilly protested. It was ridiculous, but it was still hurtful. She knew Jewish people had a range of different-sized heads, just like everyone else. It was a lie to say otherwise. But whatever she said, no one at the school, except Gretchen, would listen. She wanted to scream that they were all crazy, but the fight had gone out of her. It felt like everyone was against her.

'Inside now, children,' said Tilly's teacher, Frau Schwartz, and the children trooped in after her.

Gretchen had a long scratch down her face. Everyone who'd been in the fight looked a mess.

'We don't think Tilly should be in our class any more, miss,' one girl said.

'She's not one of us. She should go to a Jewish school,' another girl added.

'Of course you should be in our school,' Gretchen told Tilly as they took their seats. She clenched her fists and rolled her eyes at the stupidity of the girls. But Tilly knew everyone else agreed with the bullies.

Tilly looked at the photographs of Herr Hitler and his tiny moustache that stared back at her from the walls of the classroom. If anyone had a small head and small brain, it was *him*. Though she'd never dare say it out loud.

The rest of the children stood up, held out their right arm and shouted, '*Heil Hitler!*' Tilly stood up too, but she didn't give the Hitler salute because Jewish people weren't supposed to.

When everyone had sat down again, Frau Schwartz said, 'Now, today we're going to talk about careers. It'll only be a few years before you'll all be out at work.'

'We're going to join the *Führer*'s army,' one of the boys said, indicating himself and his two friends.

'I want to be a teacher like you, miss,' said a girl with her hair in pigtails.

Tilly thought of the hedgehogs she'd helped, back when they were still living in the house with a garden. She loved animals. The words slipped out of her mouth before she could stop them. 'I'd like to work with animals, miss,' she said.

'Me too!' said Gretchen.

'Maybe even one day I could train to become a vet,' Tilly added.

Frau Schwartz frowned.

'Of course *you* can't be a vet, you silly girl. People like you aren't even allowed to go to university!'

'Not in Germany, but maybe she could be a vet somewhere else, miss,' Gretchen said.

Frau Schwartz shook her head. 'I doubt that someone like Tilly would be welcome anywhere,' she replied.

Tilly swallowed hard, but in the next moment she gave a squeal of delight. The door was pushed open and her beloved Wuffly came racing into the classroom and jumped up on to her lap. Even the children who didn't like Tilly couldn't help laughing as the little dog sat there looking at the teacher.

Frau Schwartz was not impressed.

'Kindly take your dog back home, Tilly, and teach it how to behave.'

'Yes, miss,' said Tilly, standing up. She'd had enough of school for today and it was a relief to leave the classroom. 'Good dog, Wuffly,' she whispered.

Gretchen stood up too. 'I'll go with her.'

'No, you won't,' Frau Schwartz said. 'Sit down, Gretchen. It's important that pure-blooded Aryan children like you don't miss any schooling. Remember, you're our future!'

'Well, what about Tilly's future?' Gretchen asked indignantly.

Frau Schwartz sighed. 'That hardly counts. There's no need for you to come back to school today, Tilly.'

'Yes, miss.'

Tilly felt the other children staring at her as she walked past their desks with Wuffly at her heels. Some of them stuck out their tongues.

'Tilly Toadstool,' mouthed the girl she'd first attacked.

This time Tilly ignored her. She felt satisfied to see there was a big rip in the girl's blouse.

Gretchen stood up and followed Tilly. 'I'll come straight back!' she said.

'Sit back down immediately, Gretchen, or your parents will hear about this!' Frau Schwartz shouted.

Gretchen hesitated for a moment and then she sat down again as Tilly and Wuffly left the classroom.

Chapter 5

Wuffly looked up at Tilly and wagged her tail – she was very pleased with herself. She'd found her best friend and now they were outside in the fresh air and there were hundreds of interesting smells to sniff at. She was ready to play.

'You really are a *lobbus*,' Tilly said fondly as she walked out of the school gates with Wuffly almost dancing along beside her. Wuffly was the cheekiest dog ever, as well as being the sweetest and most loyal.

The dachshund wagged her tail even more. She was clearly not sorry one bit for coming into the school!

They were heading towards Grindel when Tilly had a thought. If she took Wuffly home now, the little dog would definitely be in trouble for escaping and following her, especially if Aunt Hedy was back from the community centre. Plus Frau Schwartz had said Tilly shouldn't return to school today – and it wasn't even ten o'clock. So . . . maybe they shouldn't go home just yet. She and Wuffly should go somewhere else.

Tilly smiled as she thought about the woods close to where they used to live, and the animals that resided there. One day she was going to work with animals, no matter what Frau Schwartz had said. There were hardly any animals where they lived in Grindel, apart from Wuffly and the spider – and the mice and rats. There were plenty of those.

Suddenly Tilly knew exactly where they should go.

'This way, Wuffly,' she said, and they headed off in the opposite direction to home towards Neuengamme, the neighbourhood where Tilly and her family used to live. Where Gretchen and her family *still* lived.

Soon they were surrounded by the familiar fields where she and Gretchen used to play beyond the old brickworks. They stopped at the river and Wuffly had a long refreshing drink. Tilly had loved to swim in its icy cold waters when they'd lived nearby.

Ahead of them, caught by the winter sun, she saw the glint of the metal weathervane that belonged to the residential school for deaf Jewish children.

Tilly's mum used to volunteer at the school and Tilly had gone with her sometimes. The children had been very excited when they'd realized that Tilly knew sign language too, even if she wasn't as fast or as fluent as them.

'Slower, please,' her hands would sign, when a child's hands danced in the air too quickly for her to understand.

When the headmaster of the school learnt that Tilly's grandfather was deaf too, he'd asked if the old man could pay them a visit when he and Oma next came to see Tilly and her parents.

Tilly's mum had said she was sure he'd be delighted to do so, and he was.

'Come on,' Tilly said, when Wuffly stopped to sniff at a clump of grass. The little dachshund looked up, then came running over to her as they continued towards the school.

She and her mum had both been there when Opa had told the children how he'd fought for Germany in the 1914 War.

One of the boys, a few years older than Tilly, had asked lots of questions, and as soon as Opa had answered one, his hand shot up and waved in the air to ask another.

The boy, whose name was Hans, had even followed Opa out of the school and through the small playground to ask more questions.

Finally, Tilly's mum asked the school if Hans could come to dinner with them so that he could have a chance to sign with Opa some more. Hans had come to dinner with them for the next three nights, and had been especially interested in learning how

Opa had survived in the woods alone when he'd been separated from his men.

But all that was before her mum had become ill and they'd been forced to move. There hadn't even been time to tell the deaf school they were leaving and Tilly hadn't been back there since. But now, as they neared the school building, she wished that she had.

If only everything could go back to the way it had been before. A year ago – that's where she'd like to be now.

When she and Wuffly got there, the windows of the deaf school were closed and shuttered and the place looked deserted. Tilly shivered. Maybe the Nazis had forced them to move out too. She thought of Hans and his endless questions and hoped he and the other children were OK.

'This way, Wuffly,' she said as they walked on.

A few minutes later they turned the corner and Tilly caught her breath. Just ahead of them was the house where she'd been born. Wuffly started to run excitedly towards her old home, tail wagging.

'No, Wuffly, here! *Here!*' Tilly called, and back Wuffly came.

They hid behind a tree and peered round it. Wuffly whined and sat down, looking at Tilly expectantly.

Tilly thought of the family of hedgehogs in the back garden. There had been a tame robin that used to land on her finger and sing while her dad was digging in the vegetable patch. Her dad had been happy then. 'Little robin is singing for his supper of worms,' he would joke.

Tilly hoped the hedgehogs and robin were all right. But new people must have moved into the house by now and she couldn't exactly knock on the door and ask, could she?

She was tempted, though – very tempted – to do just that. To knock and tell the new people about the hedgehogs and the robin. What harm could it do?

She gazed at the front door and bit her bottom lip. 'We don't know who's living there now,' she told Wuffly. The little dog looked up at Tilly and then back at the house and gave a wag of her tail.

But at that moment, as if answering Tilly's question, the front door of the house opened and a man dressed in a grey *Allgemeine* SS officer's uniform came out.

Tilly gasped. The *Allgemeine* SS really hated Jewish people and were responsible for enforcing the Nazis' racial policy. She was very glad she hadn't knocked on the door now.

'Come on, Wuffly,' she said, and they slipped away into the woodland before they were seen.

It had been spring the last time they'd been here and the woodlands had been full of wild flowers. But now the leaves had fallen from the trees. The birds had been singing on the day they moved to

Grindel. She hardly ever heard birds singing in town.

Tilly sat on a fallen log to share the jam sandwiches Gretchen had made for her with Wuffly. In the distance she could hear the puffing sound of a steam train passing along the railway tracks at the edge of the woods.

As she ate, she looked around. There were so many anti-Jewish laws, she didn't think anyone besides Herr Hitler could know them all. But at least Jews were still allowed to go into forests, breathe fresh air and listen to the birds singing. She couldn't help thinking, *For now.*

They'd just finished eating the sandwiches when a family of wild boars wandered past. Tilly held her breath so as not to scare them. But Wuffly started barking and the animals ran back into the trees.

'Oh, Wuffly, they were so pretty, you didn't have to frighten them!' Tilly told her.

The only laws of the Third Reich that Tilly agreed with were the ones about being kind to animals. They'd forbidden hunting on horseback, poisoning wild animals and using leghold traps.

Wuffly looked up at Tilly with her head tilted to one side, as if to say, *But scaring boars is fun!* Tilly laughed at the little dog.

'Come on,' she said, 'but no barking.' She wanted to see where the family of boar had gone. The piglets had been so sweet.

As they tramped through the woods, Tilly started to feel like she was being followed. Something felt wrong.

She heard the crack of a twig and spun round quickly to look. She couldn't see anyone – although Wuffly started growling. Most likely it was a fox or a deer. Maybe it was even the boar family. Tilly ducked behind a tree and Wuffly stayed close.

They waited there, on edge, to see if anyone came creeping up after them.

Chapter 6

From the classroom, Gretchen watched Tilly and Wuffly as they crossed the playground and went out through the school gates. She folded her arms and gave the teacher a angry look, but Frau Schwartz didn't notice.

'What about you, Carl?' Frau Schwartz said. 'What would you choose as your career?'

Gretchen sighed and looked at the empty chair beside her. School wasn't the same without Tilly there too. They'd always been in the same class, sitting next to each other, right from their very first day at kindergarten. The morning ticked past at a snail's pace.

At breaktime, outside in the frosty playground, the other children were still looking at the same stupid book that had caused the fight.

'Mushroom Mathilde's poisoned you, Gretchen; you've been infected!'

'Tilly Toadstool's toxic!'

'That's a load of rubbish!' Gretchen shouted, but no one listened to her and she felt miserable.

'Is something wrong, Gretchen?' Frau Schwartz asked when they'd gone back inside.

'They said Tilly was a poisonous mushroom,' Gretchen told her. 'It's not true. It's just a stupid book.'

'But you do know that Jewish people shouldn't be trusted,' Frau Schwartz said. 'Everyone knows that.'

Gretchen's mouth fell open. She knew that's what people said, but that didn't mean it was true. Frau Schwartz knew Tilly. She must know what she was saying wasn't true. 'But Tilly . . .'

'And *Juden* that pretend to be our friends should be trusted least of all,' the teacher continued disapprovingly.

'Tilly's not a pretend friend,' Gretchen said, shaking her head.

But Frau Schwartz wasn't even listening. 'You must choose your friends more wisely, Gretchen. Pick a new Aryan friend.'

Gretchen felt sick. Tilly was her friend and always would be.

'May I see this book that all the fuss has been about?' Frau Schwartz said to the class, and one of the children gave it to her.

Gretchen watched through narrowed eyes as the teacher turned the pages, nodding and smiling to herself every now and again.

'Tilly would never hurt any animal. She'd never hurt anyone,' Gretchen said in despair as Frau Schwartz read aloud how the kosher method of killing animals for meat was cruel.

'She kicked me this morning,' said Liesel.

'And ripped my shirt.'

'And scratched me,' said Carl, pointing to the mark down his face.

'Well I got scratched and punched and kicked too,' said Gretchen indignantly, 'and my blouse is torn at the back where someone was hanging off me!'

Frau Schwartz carried on reading bits from the book aloud.

To begin with Gretchen was angry, but when she heard more and more ridiculous things being said, she just burst out laughing.

'It's so stupid!'

But the other children weren't laughing and nor was Frau Schwartz.

'Maybe it is *you* that is the *dummkopf*, Gretchen,' she said quietly.

Chapter 7

Tilly waited and waited behind the tree until she was absolutely sure there wasn't anyone following them.

'This way,' she said to Wuffly at last.

The little dachshund immediately jumped up and wagged her tail.

They continued further into the woods and down the bank to the stream. The water was fast-flowing here, so they walked along the edge until they found a shallower bit where Wuffly could paddle.

'Oh!' Tilly said in surprise.

Close to the stream's edge, someone had made what looked like a mud snowman with pebbles for its eyes and mouth. It had a broken twig as a nose and longer twigs sticking out of the sides for arms. Two rocks had been placed where the feet should be.

Wuffly sniffed at the mud figure and circled it. Tilly grinned. It was such a funny and unexpected thing to find. She guessed some children must have made it.

She was about to take a closer look when a hand touched her lightly on the shoulder. She screamed and whirled round – and then grinned.

'Hans!'

Hans was signing at her very quickly.

'Slower, please,' Tilly signed back.

'My Golem,' Hans said, gesturing towards the mud snowman. Hans opened his mouth and then pointed inside it. Then he pointed at the Golem's mouth.

Tilly nodded. She knew the story of the Golem. To make it come to life, you had to write one of the secret magical names of God on a piece of parchment, before rolling it up and putting it in the Golem's mouth.

'Your school is closed?' Tilly signed.

Hans just shrugged. Then he picked up more clay from the riverbank, plonked it on the Golem's head and started forming it into hair.

Wuffly sniffed at the breeze. There was something very interesting not far away, something she needed to investigate. She trotted off purposefully.

Tilly went after her, and Hans stopped working on the Golem to follow them.

The dachshund quickened her step, her nose sniffing the air and then following a scent on the ground.

'Wuffly!' Tilly called, and the little dog stopped and looked back. Tilly had almost caught up with her when Wuffly wagged her tail and headed on. She was following a very interesting smell and didn't want to stop.

The little dog's nose sniffed the leafy ground, past this tree, close to the ferns, beside the warren where the rabbits lived. Wuffly panted with excitement . . . she was almost there . . . and then she wasn't.

Wuffly gave a whine of surprise and protest and sat down. She put her paw out towards the criss-crossed wire that went from the forest floor up into the sky. Beyond the wire, in the distance, she could see the German Shepherd, a potential new friend, that she'd been tracking.

Wuffly stood up and wagged her tail as she looked at the other dog.

'Where are you going, Wuffly?' said Tilly's voice behind her. 'Wait for me.'

Wuffly whined.

'What is it? What have you found?'

Tilly came to join the little dog and stared at the barbed wire dividing the woodland. Beyond the fence, all the trees had been ripped up. It wasn't a forest any more. She didn't know what it meant, or why it was there . . . but it gave her a feeling of dread.

Suddenly, there was a shrill, crackling noise that made Tilly jump. She grabbed Hans and pulled him behind a tree to hide.

'What?' Hans signed.

'Loud noise,' she signed back. She thought it must be someone speaking into a tannoy. But what was going on? Why would there be loudspeakers in a wood?

Tilly crept from tree to tree, worrying that at any moment she might be spotted by whoever had spoken. Hans and Wuffly followed closely, Wuffly's nose to the ground.

She shrank back as she saw a soldier through the trees, patrolling on the other side of the fence. He carried a gun and had a large German Shepherd dog with him.

When Wuffly spotted the dog, she started wagging her tail.

'No, Wuffly,' Tilly said in a low voice. 'Shh. This way.' She didn't want the soldier to see them, sensing they'd be in trouble if he did. The secret camp must be hidden for a reason. Why else would they have built it here among the trees?

Was *this* the real reason why her family had been forced to leave their house so quickly and move to the rented flat in Grindel?

The hidden camp looked brand new and seemed to be empty, except for whoever had spoken into the tannoy, the soldier and the dog patrolling the fence.

Now German patriotic marching music was playing over the speakers. The soldier started marching one way and then the other. He made

Hitler salutes in time to the music and then did a silly dance. The German Shepherd looked up at him as if it wasn't quite sure what was going on.

'Come on, Wuffly,' Tilly whispered. 'It isn't safe here.' She beckoned to Hans, who was grinning as he watched the soldier dancing. She knew the officer would probably be cross if he knew they'd seen him acting like a *komiker*, the word for 'comedian'.

Wuffly looked over at the German Shepherd in the distance and gave a whine.

As soon as they were a little way away, Tilly started running and Wuffly raced after her. Hans ran too, but at the edge of the woods he stopped.

'Come,' Tilly signed.

Hans shook his head. 'I stay – you go.'

Tilly frowned, shook her head and beckoned to him, but Hans refused once again. Then he disappeared into the trees as Tilly watched him go. Was he living there? Maybe he went back to the school at night. Perhaps it wasn't closed after all. It was too late to ask him now and there was nothing else she could do. They needed to go home.

Tilly and Wuffly kept close to the trees as they ran along the road beside the railway lines. They didn't stop until they were far, far away from the secret camp in the woods.

An hour later they reached the Jewish area of Grindel . . . and safety.

Chapter 8

Gretchen's mum was not at all pleased when she saw her daughter's bruises and torn clothes.

'The other children said Tilly was a toadstool!' Gretchen told her. She was late home from school because there'd been *bosseln* practice at the end of the day. Gretchen had been so angry with everyone for their unfair treatment of Tilly that she'd thrown the wooden *bosseln* ball further than she'd ever done before.

'Let the other children say what they like – it's none of your business. And *certainly* not worth getting into a fight over,' her mother said as she chopped vegetables for *bratwurst* stew. Next to her was a copy of a Nazi newspaper with headlines calling for revenge against the Jews for the shooting of the Nazi diplomat, Ernst Vom Rath.

'But she's my friend,' Gretchen said to her mother.

'Then maybe you should find a better friend.'

Gretchen sighed. She'd heard that far too many times already today.

'Looks like you've been in the wars,' Fritz said, giving his sister a friendly punch on the arm.

'Ouch – I've got a bruise there, actually!' Gretchen told him, but then she grinned because it wasn't a bad one and she was pleased her big brother was home.

'Once you're in the proper League of German Girls instead of the *Jungmädel*, no one will hurt you,' Fritz told her. 'They wouldn't dare.'

'I can take care of myself,' Gretchen said, clenching her fists.

'But not as well as the Third Reich's army will protect you!'

'Go and get changed,' Gretchen's mother told her, 'and give me your blouse. I'll see what I can do to repair it.'

After dinner, some of Fritz's friends from the Hitler Youth knocked on the door for him. They were all laughing and joking.

'Where are you going?' Gretchen asked them, but Fritz just shook his head and put his finger to his nose.

'It's not fair. Tell me. What's going on?'

'Bye, little sister,' Fritz called out as he headed for the door. 'Be good.'

'I'm going to see how Tilly is,' Gretchen said to her mother. 'The teacher sent her home with Wuffly this morning and told her not to come back.'

'No,' Mrs Schmidt said. 'You're not going anywhere tonight. You stay right here with me. In fact, you can help darn the holes in your blouse.'

Gretchen gave a loud sigh.

In Grindel, over their meatloaf and cabbage dinner, Tilly told Oma and Opa, her father and Aunt Hedy how Gretchen had said there was going to be a surprise for Jewish people coming very soon. 'She said it could be something good. Maybe the *Führer* has turned over a new leaf!'

But her family just looked worried.

'I doubt it,' said Aunt Hedy. 'Herr Hitler's making life more difficult for us every day. On the way home I saw even more shops with signs in the windows saying *No Jews*.'

Wuffly looked up at her, hoping for a crumb of meatloaf.

'Or dogs,' said Aunt Hedy. 'No Jews or dogs allowed.'

Wuffly gobbled up the small piece of meatloaf that fell from Aunt Hedy's fork.

'This can't go on,' Tilly's father said. 'Our fellow Germans must come to their senses and see that this treatment of Jewish people is all wrong.'

'We're just as German as other German people are,' Tilly said.

'There have been Jewish people living in Germany since the Middle Ages,' said Oma.

'That won't make a difference to Herr Hitler,' Aunt Hedy told them, pulling a doubtful face. 'He blames the Jews for everything and will throw us in prison, or worse, for the smallest reason.'

Maybe that is why there is a camp in the wood, Tilly thought to herself. Could it be a new prison? The existing prisons must be bursting with all of Hitler's captives.

Aunt Hedy shook her head and muttered something in Hebrew.

'No cursing at the dinner table,' Mr Abrams told her, 'however much the person may deserve it.'

'What did you say?' Tilly asked Aunt Hedy.

'That Hitler's name may be obliterated,' Aunt Hedy said.

But that wasn't very likely to happen, thought Tilly. The *Führer*'s name and the swastika flags of the Third Reich were *everywhere*.

'I'd better take Wuffly for a walk,' Tilly said when they'd all finished eating.

'Don't be long,' Aunt Hedy told her. 'It's already getting dark.'

'Careful,' signed Opa.

'I'll come with you,' Tilly's dad said.

Opa stood up from his armchair as if to come too.

'No,' Oma signed to him. 'Dangerous.'

'Why?' Tilly asked. 'Why can't Opa come?' Her grandfather almost never went out for a walk with Wuffly.

Oma looked at Tilly's dad, who gave the briefest of nods.

'Deaf people and their families are being taken by the Nazis and never seen again,' Oma said.

'What?' Tilly said, thinking of Hans. Was that why the Jewish deaf school had been shut down? Had all the children, except Hans, been taken away? Tilly was really worried about him now. She wished he'd agreed to come back here with her. 'Why?'

Oma shrugged.

'Is it only Jewish deaf people who are being taken?' Tilly asked.

'No – *anyone* who's deaf is at risk. It's because of the law for the protection of the hereditary health of German people.'

Tilly shook her head. Another law!

Opa sat down again. 'Want you safe,' he signed to Tilly.

'It's not fair,' she signed back to him. Why were people being targeted just because they were deaf? It was just as stupid as targeting people because they were Jewish. Sometimes it seemed to Tilly that the Nazis had a rule for everything – and if they hadn't thought of one yet, then they probably would by tomorrow!

'Let's go, Tilly,' said Mr Abrams. 'It's getting late.'

Tilly gave her grandfather a quick hug and then set off with her father and a very excited Wuffly.

*

'Why does the government make life so hard for us?' Tilly asked her father once they were on the street.

Mr Abrams checked no one was listening before he said, 'I think we are easy targets to blame when things go wrong. After losing the 1914 War, Germany faced many hardships. Food was blocked from coming into the country. People were starving; *children* were starving. More than half a million German people died from starvation and disease.'

'But that wasn't because of Jewish people! Didn't Jewish children and families die because of the blockade too?' Tilly said.

'Yes, of course they did,' Mr Abrams replied wearily.

'And Opa fought in that war, didn't he?'

'Yes, he did – and got a medal for doing so.'

'And lost his hearing and stopped being able to speak.'

Mr Abrams nodded. Tilly pushed her hands into the pockets of her coat. It was cold and she didn't have her gloves with her. She and her father watched Wuffly busily sniffing at one spot and then another, her tail wagging as they passed the synagogue that towered up into the sky.

'A dog's nose is more than ten thousand times as sensitive to smell as a human's,' Tilly's dad said, changing the subject.

'And their hearing is better too, isn't it?' Tilly said.

'Much better,' her dad agreed. 'That's why they don't like loud banging noises.'

They stopped outside the clothes store where Tilly's dad worked.

'It's pure vandalism,' he said, staring at the word *Jude* that had been daubed on the glass in red paint weeks ago. 'There's no point to it other than hate. Sometimes I'm glad –' He stopped in mid-sentence.

'Glad about what, Dad?' Tilly asked him.

'That your mother isn't here to see how full of hate her beloved Germany has become.'

They both fell silent at the mention of her.

'I miss her so much, Dad,' Tilly said, her voice cracking.

Her father took her hand and squeezed it. 'Me too, every single minute of every single day.'

There was the whistle of a steam train in the distance. Tilly wondered if Gretchen's father was driving it. Gretchen loved going on train journeys with him.

Tilly hoped the other children in their class hadn't picked on Gretchen after she'd gone. But then she remembered the fight in the playground. Gretchen could easily take care of herself!

'Better get back,' Tilly's father said.

There was a gang of men lurking in the shadows of a doorway just ahead. Beside them a newspaper billboard. The headline said that the

German diplomat, Ernst Vom Rath, had died from his wounds at 5.30 p.m.

'Come on, Wuffly,' Tilly said.

The little dog looked up at Tilly and her father and whined. She wanted to track the scent of a rat that had run past earlier.

'*Jude!*' one of the men shouted suddenly. '*Juden!*'

'Let's go,' said Tilly dad, grasping her hand tightly.

Wuffly looked wistfully back at the spot where the rat had gone, but then shook herself and trotted along with Tilly and Mr Abrams, who were walking very quickly indeed.

They didn't slow down until they were safely back inside their flat.

Chapter 9

It was very late and Wuffly was asleep on Tilly's bed when the sound of footsteps and voices in the distance woke her. The footsteps and voices came closer. They were followed by the sound of glass smashing. Someone screamed. More glass smashed. The voices were louder now, shouting, angry, excited voices. More screams. *Terrified* screams.

Wuffly crept up the bed and lay closer to Tilly, as close as she could get.

'It's OK, Wuffly,' Tilly said, still asleep. She put her arm round the little dog. In her dream, glass raindrops were falling from the sky.

Wuffly jumped up and gave a yap at the sound of banging on the double-fronted wooden door to the flats.

Now Tilly was awake too and rubbing at her eyes.

'What's going on?' she asked as Aunt Hedy stirred from her sleep.

'I don't know . . .'

The apartment's main door must have been opened. Downstairs, people started shouting and screaming.

'Fire!' Tilly cried, realizing she could smell smoke. She looked out of the window. Her heart raced and her eyes widened in shock. 'It's the synagogue. *The synagogue's on fire!*'

There were crowds of people out in the street, staring at the burning holy building. No one was doing anything to help!

'Why aren't the fire brigade coming?' Tilly asked wretchedly.

'Get dressed,' Aunt Hedy said.

Tilly did so hurriedly.

'It's OK, Wuffly,' she said, although she knew it wasn't true. She didn't know what was going on, but whatever it was, it definitely wasn't OK.

A moment later there was a thumping on the door of their flat. Tilly came running out of her room.

'Open up, *Juden!*' a man's voice yelled.

'Don't let them in!' Oma cried.

'Go and hide under the bed,' Aunt Hedy told her niece, but Tilly didn't.

'Little pig, little Jewish pig, let us come in!' the voice shouted, and there was more thumping on the door.

'No,' Oma begged as Mr Abrams headed towards it. '*No!*'

'Then I'll huff and I'll puff . . .' and suddenly the door burst open as booted feet kicked it in and Mr Abrams was wedged behind it.

'*Go, Mathilde!*' Aunt Hedy screamed at Tilly, but Tilly was frozen to the spot.

A mob of Nazi Brownshirts, Hitler's bullies, stormed into the flat, knocking Oma to the floor. They had members of the Hitler Youth and civilians with them.

Opa came out of the bedroom in his pyjamas, looking confused. His hair was tufted up from sleep.

The mob seized him.

'Where's your money, old man?' the leader demanded.

Tilly's grandfather couldn't understand what he was saying. The Brownshirt started shaking him roughly by the shoulders.

'Valuables – gold!' he roared. 'What are you, deaf?'

'Yes, he is! Leave him be,' cried Oma, scrabbling up from the floor where she'd been knocked and grabbing hold of the Nazi's arm.

The Brownshirt looked at her sharply. 'Deaf? Was he born deaf? Are *you* deaf?'

'No, no,' Oma protested. 'He was injured when he was fighting for Germany during the war. No one else here is deaf.'

'Just Jewish,' another Brownshirt said in disgust as he swung one arm along the fireplace, smashing all of the precious family photographs to the floor.

Tilly's grandfather made a sort of keening sound.

'Opa!' Tilly cried, running to him.

Wuffly barked and ran at the Brownshirt, but she was roughly booted aside. Then the soldier knocked Opa to the floor and kicked him.

'Leave him alone!' Tilly screamed in horror and for a moment he stopped and looked back at her, a sneer on his face.

'Why would I listen to you? Now be quiet!'

Opa crawled under the table, desperate to get away.

Tilly scooped up Wuffly, who was barking and trembling at the same time.

After that, the mob went into the bedrooms and the kitchen. Tilly could see Hitler Youth boys using their *Blood and Honour*-engraved knives to rip up the mattresses. Clothes were flung from the drawers on to the ground, ripped and stamped on. Some were thrown out of the window.

Tilly gasped in disbelief as they threw her grandfather's medal to the ground along with the photo of her mother. Everything was crushed under their boots.

'He was awarded a medal for fighting for Germany – that's why he can't speak or hear. *He's a war hero!* Why are you doing this?' she cried.

'He's no hero. He's a *Jude* and must be punished.'

'But why?'

'Shut up, little girl!'

Aunt Hedy grabbed Tilly and pulled her back. 'Hush!' she warned.

They watched helplessly as the mob smashed their glasses and ornaments and broke their furniture. Why were they doing this? Why? Even Wuffly wasn't barking any more. She was shaking with fear and watching too. The kitchen window was smashed and cutlery thrown out on to the street. The smell of burning filled the air.

The Brownshirts, some of them boys no older than Gretchen's brother Fritz, grabbed hold of Opa's legs and pulled him on his belly out from under the table.

'Leave him be,' Tilly's dad pleaded.

The Storm Trooper ordered two of the other Brownshirts to hold Mr Abrams's arms.

'You're coming with us. Resist and it will be worse for you – and your family.'

A cold icicle of fear ran through Tilly. What were they going to do to her father and grandfather?

'All of you outside – now,' the Storm Trooper commanded.

'But it's cold. Our coats . . .'

They just had time to grab their coats. Tilly helped a bewildered, shaking Opa to get his shoes on just as the Storm Trooper shouted, '*Now!*'

Chapter 10

Outside, hundreds of other Jewish people had already been corralled into the square. The men had been separated from the women and children. Everybody was just as bewildered and frightened as Tilly's family.

'What's going on?' someone asked.

'Silence!' a Brownshirt shouted.

'Why do we have to stand here?'

'No talking!' The Storm Trooper raised his gun and shot at the sky. Everyone went quiet.

Around them, smoke filled the night air, making people cough. Piles of furniture and books and clothing lay scattered all over the place.

Wuffly whined.

Tilly picked the little dog up and held her close as she stared about, wide-eyed, hardly able to take in all that was happening. It was like some unbelievable nightmare. Around her, more people screamed as they were dragged from their homes. Glass smashed and there was the never-ending choking smell of acrid smoke as books and belongings were burnt. Shops had been ransacked and everything inside was covered with water and ink, if it wasn't being set on fire.

'Armageddon!' Oma said, as Aunt Hedy tried to keep her from falling. But Oma sank to the ground. 'Armageddon!'

And Tilly thought that it really *did* feel like the end of the world.

One of the Hitler Youths who'd pulled Opa out from beneath the table stopped in front of Tilly and grabbed hold of Wuffly's collar, tearing the little dachshund from Tilly's arms.

'*No!*' Tilly cried. 'She's not yours.'

'Is now,' the boy said. 'This is much too fine a dog to belong to a *Jude!*'

Wuffly struggled to get away from the boy, but couldn't. She tried to bite him instead.

'Bad dog!' he shouted and raised his hand to hit Wuffly, but another Hitler Youth stopped him.

'The Third Reich forbids any cruelty to animals,' he warned.

But what about people? What about my father and grandfather? Tilly wanted to ask, but knew she daren't.

In the meantime, the men had been herded into a group away from the women and children, who were standing around the edges of the square.

What's going to happen to all of us? Tilly thought despairingly.

The boy sneered at Tilly and walked off with Wuffly.

'Hello, little dog. I will teach you how to be a German and not a *Jude*,' Tilly heard him say as Wuffly wriggled in his arms and barked. He pulled the name tag and the numbered dog-licence disc from Wuffly's collar, threw them to the ground and stamped on them as he strode forward.

Wuffly cried out and Tilly couldn't bear it. She tried to go after Wuffly, but her aunt grabbed her arm.

'Do you want to make it worse for your father and grandfather?' she hissed, her grasp so tight on Tilly's arm that it hurt. 'Or for Wuffly to be killed – or for you or me or Oma, for that matter?'

Tilly shook her head. She picked up Wuffly's dog-licence disc from the ground where the Hitler Youth had thrown it. The disc had been issued by the government and proved the little dachshund belonged to the Abrams family. Not that anyone in authority would probably care.

'We wait,' Aunt Hedy said as Tilly picked up Wuffly's broken name tag. 'We think rationally. Let the authorities handle it – they can't let something like this happen. They'll step in, put a stop to it. It's mob violence gone crazy. The authorities will intervene.'

But Tilly wasn't so sure. Where were the authorities to put out the fires? There was no fire brigade. She couldn't see a single uniformed regular policeman out on the street, only Hitler's men. The Brownshirt SA Storm Troopers were in charge and very much in control.

People were crying as they watched holy items being brought out of the synagogue and thrown on to pyres for burning. Tilly watched, wide-eyed, unable to believe it was all happening. Some of the *Torah*s were hundreds of years old and irreplaceable. They were always treated with reverence. Each of them had been painstakingly written in Hebrew by hand, taking two years or more, and should even one letter be damaged, the *Torah*'s holy power would be lost and it would need to be rewritten.

Then the Brownshirts made a second pile and added more prayer shawls to this one.

Worse was to come, and people around her gasped as four Storm Troopers emerged from the synagogue carrying the Ark – the large cabinet usually positioned to face Jerusalem that held the *Torah*s.

The Ark was dropped carelessly on the ground and the Storm Troopers headed back into the synagogue to see what else they could find to destroy.

'Back, stay in place, don't move!' ordered the Storm Trooper in charge of Tilly's group, waving his gun.

Tilly watched as a shadowy figure behind the Storm Trooper dashed forward, grabbed the ceremonial *shofar* from the pyre and ran off with it.

'*Hans?*' she gasped, sure she recognized him.

'Halt!' shouted the Storm Troopers coming out of the synagogue, but it was too late. The *shofar* rescuer had gone.

Aunt Hedy squeezed Tilly's hand. The *shofar* at least had been saved.

Tilly could hardly believe her eyes. It had happened so quickly.

More people came to join them, shivering in the cold. Most didn't have coats, although a few had managed to wrap blankets around themselves.

Finally, when Tilly thought it would never end and she couldn't stand up any longer, the Storm Troopers told all the women and children to go home.

'What about Father and Opa?' Tilly whispered to Aunt Hedy.

'Come,' said Aunt Hedy. 'Help me with Oma.'

They supported Oma with Tilly on one side and Aunt Hedy on the other as they staggered back to their vandalized flat. Once they were inside, Tilly ran to the window and looked out, trying to spot her father, grandfather and Wuffly in the square. But she couldn't see any of them.

Some of the men were being taken away down the street, but the Storm Troopers had most of them still in the square.

Below her she saw people holding flaming torches, using them to set fire to books, papers and clothes that had been thrown out of windows but not yet burnt.

Oma lay in Opa's broken armchair with Aunt Hedy comforting her.

'Hush, hush now,' she said, as Oma wept.

'I can smell smoke. It's close by,' Tilly said, her heart beating quickly.

'It's in the distance. Don't worry.'

Even Aunt Hedy must know how crazy her words sounded, Tilly thought. How could she not worry? How could anyone not worry?

'They won't set fire . . .' Her voice trailed off at the awfulness of what she was thinking, but Aunt Hedy knew. Aunt Hedy knew that they couldn't expect anything but hate from the Nazis.

'They wouldn't set fire to an apartment full of people. Not deliberately. They couldn't. They *wouldn't*,' Aunt Hedy said, pressing her lips together as if she were trying to convince herself.

Tilly picked up the picture of her mother from the floor. The glass was smashed, but the photograph wasn't damaged. She took it out and slipped it into her pocket.

Aunt Hedy put her arm out to Tilly and she went to join her on the floor.

She, her aunt and Oma stayed huddled there together for the rest of the night, terrified the mob might come back, sick with worry about what was happening to her father, Opa and Wuffly. Finally, achingly, and amid the chaos that was now their home, they somehow fell asleep.

Chapter 11

Wuffly looked back at Tilly as she disappeared into the night with Aunt Hedy and Oma. Why was she leaving her? Where was she going?

Wuffly tried once again to wriggle free, but the boy in the brown shirt only held on to her more tightly.

'Oh no, you don't. You're not going anywhere,' he said.

There was broken glass all over the ground. His boots made crunching sounds as he walked. The shards were illuminated by the flickering flames of torches and burning books. Men stood around a blazing bonfire warming their hands, chatting and laughing.

Wuffly and the boy followed hundreds of Jewish men being marched down the street, Tilly's father and Opa among them. Wuffly wriggled and barked as Opa stumbled and Tilly's dad stopped to help him up, only to be hit by a Storm Trooper with the end of his rifle.

'Keep moving!'

Mr Abrams held his arm over his head to protect himself from more blows. The two men staggered onwards with the rest of the group, Opa's arm round Mr Abrams's neck for support. Wuffly whined.

The boy holding Wuffly joined a crowd of his friends standing outside a cafe, with glasses of beer in their hands. They gave one to the boy and he squeezed Wuffly under his arm so he could drink it. It wasn't easy with the dog trying to wriggle free and he cursed as he spilt some of the precious beer.

'Cute dog, Otto,' one of his friends said.

'This dog was far too cute to belong to a *Jude* so I took it,' Otto told him.

Wuffly started growling.

'Doesn't look like your new dog likes you much.'

'Of course it does! What's not to like?' Otto said.

'I know that dog,' said Gretchen's brother, Fritz, coming over. 'Hey, Wuffly.'

Wuffly had met Fritz many times, back when they still lived in the big house near the woods. She gave a single wag of her tail and whined.

'Hey, Wuffly,' said Otto, who still had hold of her. 'Now I know your name. We are going to be friends, yes?'

Wuffly growled and bared her teeth.

'She's usually very gentle,' said Fritz. 'A big softy. My sister, Gretchen, always plays with her. Every

Christmas she asks my parents if she can have a dog just like her.'

'Um . . . do you want it?' Otto said, staring at Wuffly's sharp white teeth. With the dog still growling at him, he wasn't sure that he wanted her after all. 'What's she worth to you?'

'I'll give you this bottle of schnapps in exchange,' said Fritz.

'Done!' said Otto, taking the bottle of schnapps and immediately swigging from it.

Fritz tied some string he had in his pocket round Wuffly's red-and-gold collar so she couldn't escape. Everyone seemed tired but happy from their night's adventures. Wuffly whined and looked miserably from one boy to another as they congratulated themselves.

'The night of the broken glass – I'll never forget it.' '*Kristallnacht*.'

'Now the *Juden* will know we mean business. Now they will know that they're not welcome in Germany any more. Now they know what happens if one of them *dares* to kill a Nazi diplomat!'

At long last Fritz headed home with Wuffly.

'Gretchen is going to be very pleased to see you,' he said.

Wuffly didn't wag her tail.

Chapter 12

It was just starting to get light, but still very early when Tilly woke. For a second she wondered why she was sleeping on the hard floor instead of her bed – and then gasped as she remembered what had happened. Her father and Opa ... and Wuffly.

It was freezing inside the flat, but outside it would be much worse. Opa and her father must be so cold and tired. Tilly bit her bottom lip. She couldn't get over how Opa had been manhandled by the Hitler bullies – as if he didn't deserve to be treated any better. But he *did* deserve to be! Everyone did. He was her Opa and she loved him.

Tilly looked over at Aunt Hedy and Oma huddled together, still asleep.

Then she carefully moved the chairs away from the front door and let herself out.

As she walked down the stairs she could hear weeping from the other flats.

'Why?' a voice wailed. 'Why?'

The big main door to the apartment block had been torn off. On the street, people were clearing up broken glass from windows and shopfronts. Tilly thought they seemed to be moving in slow motion as if they were in shock. She felt like she was in shock too, as if the awfulness of last night couldn't have been real. But it *was* real – it had really happened. Really, really happened.

'Do you know where the Jewish men were taken last night?' she asked Mrs Jacobs, who was sweeping up glass.

'The police station, maybe,' Mrs Jacobs said. She had black circles under her eyes. 'Only there were so many . . .' She shook her head. 'They'll never be able to fit them all in.'

'No,' agreed Tilly.

'And people are still being arrested,' Mrs Jacobs called after her. 'Be careful. It isn't over yet!'

Tilly raced to the police station, but when she got there she found crowds of other people who had the same idea.

'Most of the Jewish men arrested last night are going to KolaFu,' a portly policeman told everyone.

'What's KolaFu?' Tilly asked the lady next to her, who had started to weep at the policeman's words.

'There were too many arrests for everyone to be held here,' the policeman continued.

'It's short for Fuhlsbüttel concentration camp,' the woman sobbed.

'The place has been run by the *Gestapo* since 1936. It's reputation for cruelty is legendary,' someone else added.

Tilly felt sick. Her dad and Opa *couldn't* be sent there.

'Seven hundred *Juden* will be interred at KolaFu for a short time before being released or sent on to other camps by truck or train,' the policeman said. 'Other troublemakers are being taken to Sachsenhausen camp.'

'Where's that?' Tilly asked.

'Not far from Berlin,' someone told her. Berlin was more than three hours away by train.

Tilly left the police station feeling utterly miserable. She had to tell Aunt Hedy and Oma what she had found out. Maybe Aunt Hedy could ask the Jewish community centre for help. There must be something someone could do.

She was worried about Wuffly too, but she didn't think the Hitler Youth boy would hurt the little dog, especially not after she'd heard them say that cruelty to animals was forbidden.

'Hey you, *Jude* girl!' a voice shouted. There was a gang of boys behind her. They were dressed in brown Hitler Youth uniforms.

Tilly pretended she hadn't heard them, but quickened her step.

'Stop when I tell you to!'

Tilly thought it was definitely *not* a good idea to stop. She heard footsteps chasing after her and didn't dare look over her shoulder.

She started running. There was a bakery just ahead. She ran in through the door and the bell rang. 'Some boys,' she gasped to the man behind the counter. 'They're after me.'

'*Jude?*' the shop owner asked.

Tilly nodded, eager for his help.

'No *Juden*,' the man said, pointing to the sign in the window.

'But . . .'

'No *Juden*,' the man repeated firmly, indicating the door.

Tilly's shoulders slumped as she turned and slowly walked towards it.

As she left the shop, she was relieved to see the street clear of her pursuers. A moment later, though, she discovered she had misjudged the situation as one of the Hitler Youth boys grabbed her from behind.

Tilly screamed. There were people walking past, but no one came to help.

'Help, help me! *Please! Help!*'

She struggled to get away, but another boy held on to her too and she couldn't escape. A third boy pulled out his Hitler Youth *Blood and Honour-*engraved knife and for a moment Tilly truly thought he was going to kill her. Her family didn't even know where she was – and now she'd be left for dead in the street. After last night she was pretty sure that whatever the Hitler Youth did, they wouldn't be punished for it.

But the boy didn't use his knife to kill her. He grabbed hold of her long plait in his fist and sliced it off.

'Look at me!' he shouted as he waved her cut hair in circles high above his head.

The next moment a shoe came flying through the air and hit him on the back of the head. It knocked him over. The other two boys let go of Tilly as they went to help their friend scramble to his feet.

Tilly knew what she had to do. She ran for her life, faster than she'd ever run before.

Chapter 13

Gretchen was amazed to find Wuffly lying on her bedroom floor when she woke up.

'What are you doing here?' she asked the little dog, and then laughed when Wuffly ran over to her and jumped up on to her bed. 'It's very nice to see you too, but why are you here?' Gretchen said, pushing back the covers.

Fritz, her mother and father were in the kitchen eating breakfast.

'Why's Wuffly here?' Gretchen asked as her mother put a plate of sausages and eggs down on the table for her.

'Wuffly's your dog now,' Fritz said round a mouthful of blood sausage. 'She was confiscated from the Abramses last night.'

'Confiscated – but why?' Gretchen asked.

She saw the look between her mother and father.

'The Jews caused a lot of trouble last night,' her mother said. 'They deliberately set fire to their own shops and threw their belongings into the streets.

They even tried to set the synagogue on Bornplatz on fire – but only managed to ruin the inside of it.'

Gretchen scratched her head.

'But why?' she asked. It didn't make sense.

'Who knows what goes on in a *Jude*'s head,' said her father, 'but they'll be punished for their behavior and made to pay for the damages.'

'And rightly so,' said her mother.

Wuffly looked at Gretchen and whined. Gretchen gave her a bit of sausage and Wuffly gobbled it up.

Gretchen smiled as she watched the little dog eating. But then she said, 'I can't keep Wuffly. I'll have to take her back to Tilly.'

Fritz shook his head.

'Wuffly's yours now. One of the other Hitler Youths took her from Tilly, but I got Wuffly back so you could have her – in exchange for a bottle of schnapps. Be a bit more grateful!'

Wuffly looked at Gretchen's plate, hoping for another bite of sausage.

Gretchen obliged. 'Here you are.'

Her mother frowned. 'I don't know how I feel about having a *Jude* dog living with us. Why don't you have a nice German Shepherd puppy instead?' she said.

Gretchen's eyes widened. She'd love a German Shepherd puppy and had been asking for one for ages, but she needed to give Wuffly back to Tilly first.

She slipped out of the house with the little dog when no one was looking.

Wuffly had been in the basket of Tilly's bicycle a long time ago, but Tilly hadn't gone nearly as fast as Gretchen pedalled. Wuffly's fur flew back as they raced through the icy-cold morning air.

'Tilly's going to be so pleased to have you back!' Gretchen said as she rode.

As they got closer to the Jewish area, the devastation of last night became apparent. Gretchen slowed down, aghast at what she was seeing. Homes daubed with paint, doors kicked in, windows smashed and glass everywhere. In some places there were clothes all over the road, some covered in ink. Cutlery, plates, cups and saucers. She had to get off her bike and walk because there was so much debris she couldn't cycle through it.

And the people – some of them bleeding, some of them walking around, eyes glazed. Others seemed excited, gazing around at the chaos.

As she passed the shop where Tilly's dad worked, she saw that it had almost been torn down. The shopfront had been smashed and the clothes inside it covered in ink and water. There were bits of paper everywhere, blowing in the wind and on the ground.

The shop owner came out of the broken front door. He looked at Gretchen in despair.

'Thirty years I've had this store,' Mr Rubenstein said. 'Thirty years and it's gone in one night. For no reason at all.'

'I'm sorry,' Gretchen tried to say as she made her way forward, but he didn't seem to hear her.

SS guards with rifles were walking Jewish men down the street towards the train station.

'Move along there!'

Were these worried, frightened-looking men the ones who had caused all the trouble? Gretchen wondered. Could it really be true?

Wuffly wanted to get out of the basket, but Gretchen told her no. 'It's too dangerous. I don't want you getting your paws cut.'

Ahead of them she could hear people jeering and shouting. As they turned the corner Gretchen saw crowds of people throwing stones at the beautiful stained-glass windows of the synagogue. As the last of its windows smashed, the vandals cheered with delight.

How can anyone think this is worth cheering about? Gretchen thought, but she didn't say anything. She didn't want the crowd to turn on her.

Behind them there was the rumble of a lorry. She and Wuffly looked over to see a truck full of defeated-looking Jewish men being driven past. It was followed by another truck and another and another.

Wuffly barked and jumped out of the bicycle basket.

'No Wuffly, come back!' Gretchen called. She got on her bike and started pedalling after the little dog.

Wuffly ran down a side street towards a group of Hitler Youth boys. An icy feeling of dread ran through Gretchen when she saw that they were holding a panicked and frightened Tilly, who was struggling to get away from them.

'Look at me!' one of the boys shouted as he waved Tilly's severed plait above his head.

Still on her bicycle, Gretchen reached down and pulled off one of her shoes. As she cycled past she threw it as hard as she could at the boy holding Tilly's plait and knocked him to the ground. The other two boys let go of Tilly and she ran off as they went to help their friend.

'Who did that?'

'Who dared to?'

'You'll pay!'

But Gretchen was gone.

Wuffly ran down the street after Tilly, but her short legs couldn't quite catch up as she raced away.

They both dashed in through the open gap where the apartment block door had been, Wuffly a moment after Tilly.

Aunt Hedy and Oma were doing their best to sort out the chaos of their ransacked flat when Tilly and Wuffly arrived, panting.

'Tilly! Why did you cut your beautiful hair?' Aunt Hedy gasped.

'I didn't. I had it sliced off by some Hitler Youth with his Hitler knife.' There were tears in Tilly's eyes. Now that she was home, her whole body started shaking.

Aunt Hedy's face went white. Oma started weeping.

'They could have killed you,' Aunt Hedy said.

Tilly swallowed hard. If it hadn't been for that shoe someone had thrown at the boys, they might well have done.

'It's OK,' Tilly said, touching the empty space where her long hair had been with still-shaking hands. 'I'm not hurt, not badly – just bruises; and my hair will grow again. And look – we've got Wuffly back!' She knew she was going to be really upset about her hair at some point, and this morning she'd truly thought she was going to be killed. But now Wuffly was home. Tilly didn't know how Wuffly had found her, but she was very glad she had. All they needed now was for her father and Opa to come home too.

But the fact that Tilly wasn't badly hurt didn't seem to soothe Aunt Hedy at all . . . and having Wuffly back didn't seem to help, either.

'But *why* is she back? Are they going to come looking for her? Are they going to come back here?' she wanted to know.

Tilly shook her head. She didn't have an answer. 'Wuffly was just there suddenly, running along behind me.'

'She's very good at escaping,' Oma said, looking at Wuffly. 'Dachshunds are smart, but your dog's the smartest one I've ever met – as well as sometimes being the most stubborn and determined. If any dog could escape from anywhere it would be her!'

Wuffly looked up at Tilly and wagged her tail as if she were agreeing with Oma.

'If she did escape, they'll be angry. They'll come after her,' Aunt Hedy said, her eyes wide with fear. 'She's their dog now. They know where Wuffly lives, where we live. If they find us harbouring her – well, God help us; and your father and grandfather, what about them? We don't even know what's happened to them – or if they're even still alive. *Dummkopf!*' She started crying, great loud noisy sobs.

'They won't find her,' Tilly said, determined not to cry. She had to be strong for her family and for Wuffly. 'I'll keep her hidden. No one will know she's here.' She knelt down and stroked Wuffly's fur while Oma patted Aunt Hedy on the back until she eventually stopped sobbing.

Tilly went into her bedroom with Wuffly.

Last December, her mother had given her a beautiful big silver locket in the shape of a heart for her birthday. Fortunately, the Brownshirts hadn't found it when they'd devastated the flat. The locket didn't have a picture in it yet, but it did have a little piece of heart-shaped card. Tilly carefully wrote Wuffly's name on the card and put it back inside the locket along with Wuffly's government-issued numbered disc. There was no point putting the broken name tag in too.

She heard the front door close and when she came out of her bedroom, she found that Aunt Hedy had gone.

'She's going to the Jewish community centre to see if they have any news of your father and Opa,' Oma told her.

Tilly nodded as she helped Oma to clear up their smashed possessions.

Wuffly trotted into the kitchen to see if the mouse that lived under the stove wanted to come out and play. But the mouse's nocturnal routine had been spoilt by the rumpus of last night and it wasn't in the mood for fun.

Chapter 14

When Gretchen arrived home from Grindel, Fritz wanted to know why Wuffly wasn't with her.

'Where's the little *Jude* dog?' he said.

'She went running after Tilly,' Gretchen told him.

'*Dummkopf*,' Fritz said, shaking his head. 'Wuffly will just get taken away from her again – only this time it could be worse for Tilly and her family.'

Gretchen bit her bottom lip and looked worried. 'But Wuffly's her dog,' she said.

'I need to go to work now,' Mr Schmidt said, coming into the kitchen, 'but at least they'll pay overtime.'

'Good,' said Mrs Schmidt. 'It's only fair that they do.'

'I know, only I'm not sure how I'm going to manage now Aldo's off work with a broken leg,' Mr Schmidt said. 'I need someone to load the engine with coal. I've only got two hands.'

Gretchen loved going on the train with her father, and he'd taken her and Fritz with him whenever he could. Although, of course, it was strictly against the rules.

'I'll load the coal,' she said. 'Go on, Dad, you know I can do it.'

'I'm coming too,' Fritz said, although Gretchen thought he still looked half asleep from being out last night with his friends.

She grabbed her coat.

'No, Gretchen,' said her mum. 'You shouldn't go. I need help here.'

'I'm going!' Gretchen insisted.

'Me too,' said Fritz.

'Let's go, then,' Mr Schmidt said.

'You spoil them,' Gretchen's mother called after him.

But Gretchen didn't agree. 'We're helping Dad!' she called back.

Frau Schmidt sighed.

When they got to the station, Gretchen saw lots of men waiting in the third-class passenger carriages of the train. Some of them were sitting on the wooden benches, but there wasn't room for everyone, so some people were standing up or sitting on the floor.

On the platform there were lots of soldiers with rifles.

'Why's the train so crowded?' she asked, but her father didn't answer.

'This way,' he said, and Gretchen and Fritz followed him down the platform to the front of the train.

'I want to be a train driver when I grow up,' Gretchen said, but Fritz laughed and shook his head.

'There aren't any women train drivers,' he said. 'Just men.'

'Then I'll be the first!' Gretchen told him. 'I'd make a better train driver than you. Why's the train so full, Dad –' she asked again, but Fritz interrupted.

'I don't want to be a train driver,' he declared. 'I want to be a dog soldier for the *Führer*.'

'Just make sure you keep shovelling the coal in,' their dad told them. 'It's a long way to Sachsenhausen.'

Gretchen frowned. It wasn't safe to have a train so overcrowded with people. Everyone should have a seat, especially on a long trip. Why were there so many men and no women or children on board?

'What's at Sachsenhausen?' she asked.

'A labour camp where the Jewish troublemakers from last night will be spending their time making bricks,' her father told her.

'Oh!' Gretchen said. So that's who the passengers on the train were.

'Don't worry, there's lots of soldiers to make sure they behave,' Fritz said.

Gretchen wasn't exactly sure why the Jewish troublemakers had done what they'd done, but she'd seen the smashed glass and the property damage. There was going to be an awful lot of cleaning up to do.

Three hours later they arrived at Sachsenhausen.

As soon as her dad stopped the train, Gretchen jumped off. She wanted to see what the *Juden* troublemakers looked like. She stayed behind the line of soldiers, though, because they had their guns pointed at the train, ready, and she didn't want to be shot at by mistake.

Gretchen's mouth fell open as one of the train doors was unbolted and she watched the 'troublemakers' stumble out. They didn't look at all like she'd imagined. Lots of them were old, some looked like they'd been beaten up, others looked bewildered.

Then Gretchen saw Tilly's grandad.

'Opa!' she said, shocked.

The old man stumbled as he got off the train. One of the soldiers pushed him with a rifle to hurry him along and he fell on to the platform.

'No!' Gretchen cried, running over to him. 'That's Tilly's opa – don't hurt him. Please don't hurt him. He's not a troublemaker! You've made a mistake.'

The soldier in charge looked over at her.

'Who are you?' he said angrily. 'This is none of your business. Civilians shouldn't be here.'

'My dad drove the train.'

She looked at Tilly's grandad – he was signing to her as he lay on the ground.

'Tell Tilly I love her.'

Gretchen nodded. 'I'll tell her. I'll tell her you love her,' she promised as the old man was hoisted up and dragged away.

'Time we were going,' said Gretchen's father, taking her arm.

'Why is the girl behaving like this?' the soldier wanted to know. 'She is not patriotic.'

'No, no, she is,' Gretchen's father said quickly. 'Very patriotic, as is her brother. He is part of the Hitler Youth.'

Fritz gave the Hitler salute.

'And the girl – is she a League of German Girls member?' the soldier said.

'No, she's not old enough yet; she's part of the Young Girls' League, though – and she will be part of the League of German Girls soon,' Gretchen's father told him.

'If you bring her again, make sure she is wearing her uniform or she might end up going to the camp with the *Juden*,' the soldier said as he turned away from them.

Her father nodded to the soldier's back. 'Hurry, Gretchen,' he said, pushing her along.

Behind her she heard a gunshot. The sound of it went through her and she tried to look round.

'No!' her father yelled, holding Gretchen so she couldn't see what had happened. 'Don't look. You don't want to know.'

'You have to join the League of German Girls now,' Fritz said seriously as they got back on the train.

'If you don't, our whole family could be sent to the camp,' said Mr Schmidt, looking very worried. 'It's not a game any more, Gretchen. This is serious. Deadly serious.'

'But how could Tilly's grandad be a troublemaker?' Gretchen was desperate to know. 'What could he have done?'

Fritz shrugged. 'Best not to question authority,' he said. 'It's best just to obey.'

Gretchen bit her lip and gazed at her big brother. She'd always looked up to him, but was blind obedience really the best way? She didn't think so.

As she and Fritz loaded the coal and the train steamed back to Hamburg, she couldn't get the awful image of Tilly's grandad out of her head.

'Why?' she asked her father and brother. 'Why did they treat Opa like that? What could he have done that was so bad? Why did they have to put him in a camp? Where's Tilly's dad? Do you think he was there too?'

But they didn't have any answers.

'Gretchen, I've decided if you promise to behave and stop making a fool of us all with your Jewish support, you can have a dog. A puppy,' Mr Schmidt told her as the train headed homewards.

Gretchen's eyes opened wide.

'A dachshund like Wuffly?'

'No, you want a bigger dog – a German Shepherd, or a Dobermann, or even a Rottweiler,' Fritz told her.

Gretchen frowned. 'But I love Wuffly.'

'Remember, there are conditions.'

'The League of German Girls?'

'Yes. You must join as soon as you're old enough.'

'It's the patriotic thing to do,' Fritz said.

Sometimes the League of German Girls and the Hitler Youth marched down the streets carrying banners and beating drums.

'You should be part of this,' Gretchen's mum had said when she and Gretchen had gone to watch. 'You should make us proud like your brother.'

'We'll talk more about this later,' her dad told her, looking very serious as the train pulled into Hamburg. 'I've got paperwork to fill in.'

As Gretchen and Fritz passed the two stone lions that guarded the entrance to the train station, she saw many Jewish men being marched inside, surrounded by armed guards.

'Where are they taking them?' she heard a lady ask.

'To a work camp,' someone else told her. 'They deserve it – one of them shot one of ours, after all.'

'They're the troublemakers who started all this last night. Foolish *Juden* smashing up their own shops and property.'

'Who does that?' someone else said. '*Dummkopfs*.'

'They should be made to pay for the clean-up.'

'We could get injured walking on all this broken glass.'

'It's not their fault. I heard their brains are a different size from ours. Smaller, inferior.'

That's a load of rubbish! Gretchen wanted to shout. *Racist rubbish!* But she didn't, because now she was frightened. Frightened of what could happen if she spoke out. Would she be put in prison too – just for having a Jewish friend? Before she'd have laughed at the idea, but now she wasn't sure. She really wasn't sure at all.

Chapter 15

'I have to go,' Gretchen said to her brother Fritz.

She had to tell Tilly and her family the awful news about Opa. All she could see was his poor bruised face and his wrinkled old hands signing that he loved his granddaughter. All she could hear was the sound of a single gunshot and all the questions it raised. She had to deliver his message.

Fritz nodded. He too had been shocked by the sight of the defenceless old man lying on the station platform.

'See you at home,' he said as she headed off in the opposite direction.

Gretchen's usual jolly knock on Tilly's door consisted of three quick raps followed by two slow. But today her heart was too heavy with the terrible news she had to deliver, so she gave three slow ones and two very slow.

Tilly opened the door cautiously. Wuffly, who was supposed to stay in Tilly's room, came rushing out, wagging her tail at the sight of Gretchen.

'Gretchen, what are you doing here?' Tilly asked her.

'I had to tell you . . .' A tear ran down Gretchen's face and she brushed it away with her fingers. Wuffly sat on the floor and looked up at her, head tilted to one side.

Tilly had never seen Gretchen cry before and knew something must be really wrong.

'What's happened? What is it?' she asked her friend. 'Come inside.'

Gretchen went into the kitchen where Oma was.

'Gretchen?' Oma said. 'What are you doing here?'

'I have very bad news,' Gretchen said. She gulped as another tear slipped down her face. More tears followed. 'My father transported the men. The ones who caused trouble during the night of the broken glass – *Kristallnacht* – to Sachsenhausen prison camp this morning on the train. Your grandfather was one of the men he took.'

'Opa? Is he OK?' Tilly asked.

Just from looking at Tilly, Gretchen knew what she was thinking – *had Mr Schmidt been able to help her father and Opa? And if not, why hadn't he?*

'When's Opa coming home?' said Oma, grabbing Gretchen's arm.

'Was my dad with him?' said Tilly.

All Gretchen could do was shake her head, over and over. *I don't know*, to every question.

'Fritz and I went with my dad. Opa sent you a message,' she told Tilly, and then made the signs exactly as Opa had done. 'He was lying on the ground. The soldiers had guns. I didn't see, but I heard . . . I heard a shot.'

'*Get out!*' Oma screamed suddenly at Gretchen. 'Get out! Never come back. Get out! Get out!' And then she said the word Jewish people used to describe non-Jews they didn't like. '*Goy!*'

Oma's exclamations were still ringing in the air when the front door opened and Aunt Hedy came rushing in.

'I have news!' she said. Her face was flushed with excitement.

'About Dad?' Tilly asked.

'About Opa?' asked Oma.

Aunt Hedy shook her head and then did a double take. 'Gretchen, what are you doing here?' she asked.

'She's just leaving!' said Oma, giving Gretchen a fierce look.

Gretchen's face turned red with embarrassment. 'I just brought bad news,' she said softly.

'Yes, you did!' said Oma.

'What news?' Aunt Hedy asked anxiously.

The others relayed the awful information.

86

'You'd better go,' Aunt Hedy finally said to Gretchen.

'I thought you should know as soon as possible,' Gretchen said to Tilly, whose face had gone a sickly white.

'Why couldn't you have done something to stop it?' Tilly said. 'Why couldn't you have helped him? Done something? Done *anything*? *Why*?'

'It's because of you coming here all the time that he was taken in the first place!' Oma screamed as Gretchen made her way towards the front door. '*The Gestapo took him because of you!*'

'I'm sorry,' Gretchen said to Tilly. Her friend looked wretched. 'I understand that it's –'

'You *don't* know what it's like!' Tilly shouted and Gretchen flinched. 'You don't understand anything! What it's like to be hated by just about everyone you meet. To be continually picked on and bullied. To have your grandfather and dad taken away! You live your perfect life in your perfect house and you don't understand *anything*!'

Gretchen was so shocked that she didn't know what to say.

'I don't want to be friends any more,' Tilly said. 'Just go, Gretchen.'

'But –'

'*Go!*' Oma screamed, her shrill voice full of pain and anger.

Gretchen walked out of the door and Tilly slammed it after her.

As she stood on the landing, Gretchen saw the door of the neighbouring flat open a crack. Had they heard her being screamed at? Being told to go away? She'd never seen Tilly like this before . . . so full of rage.

Gretchen realized her hands were shaking. Her stomach felt hollow. She looked back at the closed door. There was no point trying to reason with Tilly or her family. She'd come with such terrible news, she didn't blame them for hating her. She'd never forget the look on Oma's face. Never, ever.

Another door opened as she passed. Gretchen glanced over nervously. Was there a spy in there? Were they going to report her to the *Gestapo*? Was she really the reason Opa and Tilly's father had been taken to Sachsenhausen? She couldn't have been, she reasoned with herself. It didn't make sense, but still the doubt remained as she headed back down the stairs. The walls of the apartments here were so thin she could hear voices coming from most of them. How many of these homes had spies living inside?

For as long as she'd been able to read there had always been posters on walls and lamp posts asking people to report anything suspicious, but Gretchen hadn't paid much attention. Now she truly saw them for what they were and it made her shudder.

The Germany she loved seemed to have disappeared and in its place was a dark, scary world full of suspicion and hate.

When Gretchen had gone, Aunt Hedy turned to Tilly.

'Are you OK?' she asked gently.

Tilly nodded her head slowly, though she was lying. She wasn't OK.

'What were you going to say when you came in?' Tilly asked.

Aunt Hedy looked over at Oma, who was curled up, almost hugging herself, and weeping.

'The Jewish community centre says there's a chance for you to escape Germany and go to live in England, where you will be safe,' she said softly. Her previous excitement was now dulled by the news she had just heard.

'I don't –' Tilly started to say, but Aunt Hedy continued.

'The British government is being pressed to take ten thousand Jewish children – only children, mind. Obviously, there are far more than ten thousand Jewish children under Hitler's regime that are in need of safety, but I put your name down. They are taking orphans first, and I think maybe because of you having no mother . . . well, I think you'd have a good chance of being picked. The rescue is being organized by the Jews and a group called the Quakers.'

'The Quakers?' Tilly asked.

'They're good people who want to help us. And thank goodness for Britain, because most other countries are saying no to Jewish people, even though the whole world must surely be horrified after what happened here last night. How could they not?'

'But I don't want to leave,' Tilly said. Germany was her home. She'd never even been out of the country before and now Aunt Hedy wanted her to go away all on her own. She couldn't just leave the family, especially when they needed her. How would they manage? And she certainly didn't want to leave Wuffly behind.

She leant down to give the little dachshund a stroke. She *never* wanted to be separated from Wuffly.

'I'll never leave you,' Tilly promised.

Aunt Hedy looked deflated. She rubbed at her temple like she had a headache. 'Well, we don't know if you'll be accepted yet. Not everyone who applies to go will be chosen, but those who are . . . will be the fortunate ones. Who knows what terrible fate lies in store for everyone else.' She paused and looked over at Oma, who was clasping Opa's war medal to her. Then she turned back to Tilly and said softly, 'Now why don't you help me make everyone some *kugel* soup?'

Fritz and Mr and Mrs Schmidt were eating apple strudel when Gretchen got home.

'What's going on?' she asked suspiciously. They never usually ate strudel cake in the middle of the day.

'We're celebrating your clever brother,' Mrs Schmidt said.

'I've been accepted at one of the Adolf Hitler Schools,' Fritz told her, and Gretchen's eyes widened. The AHS were twelve elite boarding schools run by the SS.

'He was chosen following the two-week selection process at the camp he was on,' Mrs Schmidt said. She was so proud of Fritz that it might as well have been her who had been chosen, Gretchen thought.

'Where do you have to go?' she asked Fritz. She hoped it wasn't too far away because as much as he teased her, she knew she'd miss him.

'Berlin,' Fritz told her, and Gretchen frowned. Berlin felt too far away.

'I'll be travelling there with him and staying for a few days to make sure he's settled in,' Mrs Schmidt went on.

'You don't need to do that,' Fritz said.

'I most certainly do,' she told him. 'Today will go down in history as the proudest moment in the lives of the Hamburg Schmidts.'

Chapter 16

There was a soldier with a gun standing outside the gates when Tilly arrived at school on Friday morning.

Breathe and act naturally, Tilly told herself. She was feeling awkward about seeing Gretchen again. Embarrassed about what had been said. But she'd been so angry when she'd heard what had happened to Opa. Now, in the cold light of day, she realized there was nothing Gretchen could really have done to help. There was probably nothing anyone could have done. It felt like a grey cloud was floating above her wherever she walked. A grey cloud that wouldn't go away however upset or angry she felt and however much she cried.

The last time she'd been at school, on Wednesday, she'd been sent away when Wuffly arrived. That day felt like a very long time ago now after everything that had happened. Almost like a different lifetime.

She forced herself to walk through the school gates, past the soldier standing there, although her hands were shaking so much she had to put them in her pockets so he wouldn't see and be suspicious. What if the soldier on guard stopped her? What if he put her in prison for no reason other than being Jewish?

But the soldier didn't say anything. And Tilly realized it was because he was probably not even aware that she was a Jewish girl. How would anyone know unless they were told? Jewish people looked just the same as everyone else – because they *were* the same as everyone else!

Tilly breathed a sigh of relief as she walked on through the playground to the main entrance. The headmaster stood at the door, waiting for her, it seemed.

'Jewish children are not being taught here any more. You must leave immediately,' he said. He sounded frightened and kept looking over at the soldier as he spoke.

'But how am I supposed to learn?' Tilly said.

The headmaster shook his head sadly, she thought.

'Goodbye, Mathilde. Please don't come back here. It will only cause trouble.'

As Tilly walked out of the school gates, past the soldier, she looked back at the windows and saw the other children staring at her. Some of them seemed to be jeering. Tilly swallowed hard. How could they? How could they treat another person as if they didn't matter? How could they laugh at someone else's suffering? *I won't let them see I'm upset*, she thought, making her way out with her back straight and chin held high.

But once the children couldn't see her any more, she broke into a run, the tears streaming down her face. She wanted to get away from the school now. Get away and never come back.

A few minutes later, Gretchen arrived at school.

'Where's Tilly?' she asked, seeing the empty seat in the classroom.

'As of today, Jewish children are officially no longer welcome at this school,' Frau Schwartz told her smugly.

'Good,' one child said. 'She didn't belong.'

Gretchen stared down at the top of her desk and didn't say anything. She knew her classmates were wrong about Tilly. But now Tilly didn't even want to be her friend any more, all the fight had gone out of her. She just felt sad.

Wuffly was delighted when Tilly came home early and ran round in little circles of happiness. She looked so funny that Tilly had to smile, even though she felt confused and sad.

'You'll go to a Jewish school instead,' Aunt Hedy said. 'It'll be much safer for you. And you'll be with children of your own kind, rather than children that have been brainwashed by Hitler.'

Tilly nodded, but she was going to miss her old school. She and Gretchen had always been to the same one ever since kindergarten. They'd become friends on their very first day there and had remained friends ever since. Although Tilly wasn't quite sure Gretchen was her friend any more. Not after the last time they'd seen each other. Not after what had been said.

Tilly shook her head as she remembered and felt angry again.

She'd never forgive Gretchen or Mr Schmidt or Fritz. They should have done something. They should have helped Opa.

Tilly ran her fingers through her short hair. Was her dad even with Opa? Was Opa still alive? Every time she thought about it she had a terrible sinking feeling in her stomach. She didn't want to believe that the shot Gretchen heard was aimed at Opa. Gretchen hadn't actually seen what happened, after all. Didn't know for sure . . . The terrible sinking feeling crept up to her throat. She didn't know, but she hoped fervently that Opa was all right. She hoped he was with her father and that she'd see them again soon.

Tilly bit her bottom lip. At the police station the policeman had mentioned two concentration camps that Jewish men were being sent to. She hoped her father and Opa hadn't been separated.

In Grindel, they didn't call what had happened *Kristallnacht* like the Nazis did. 'Crystal Night' or the 'Night of the Broken Glass' was too pretty a description for the devastation that had occurred. Tilly's remaining family, and other Jewish people, called it 'the pogrom'. Pogroms were violent riots or massacres and destruction against religious groups – and that was exactly what had happened.

'Of course we'll still have the special Friday evening meal tonight as we've always done,' Aunt Hedy said when Tilly asked her. 'We must try to keep the *Shabbat* now more than ever!'

Tilly nodded, but the *Shabbat* was about family and two of theirs had been taken from them. Her heart ached. She missed her father and Opa so much. She could barely think for worrying about them.

'Help me lay the table,' Aunt Hedy said.

This Sabbath meal did not have the usual white tablecloth or napkins because they'd been thrown out of the window by the Hitler Youth. But Aunt Hedy had brought home some *challah*, beautiful traditional braided bread, from the Jewish community centre.

Wuffly sniffed at the scent of the freshly made loaf.

The candles had all been broken, but one half-candle was still usable.

Aunt Hedy was just about to light it when there was a knock at the door.

'Who is it?' Oma called out nervously.

Tilly half-expected the door to be kicked in by some soldier's booted foot.

'Me,' replied Mr Abrams, his voice sounding tired and weak.

Tilly rushed to the door and pulled it open with Wuffly right behind her.

Her father's head had been shaved and he no longer had a beard. His face was very bruised and his left eye was half-closed and purple. Alongside, helping him to stand, was another man that Tilly recognized from the synagogue. His head was shaved too.

'Papa!' Tilly cried, laughing with relief and crying at the same time. She threw her arms round him. Her dad swayed slightly with the weight of her, so Tilly hugged him a little less tightly.

'We're so pleased you're home – so, so pleased,' said Aunt Hedy.

The man said he couldn't stay and had better be getting back.

'Thank you, Benjamin,' Mr Abrams said to him and the man nodded once.

'I still can't believe it. Have they released everyone?' Aunt Hedy asked.

Mr Abrams shook his head as he stretched out a hand to stroke Wuffly's soft fur. 'Only those of us who promised, on our lives, that we would leave Germany. I swore I would apply for visas to every country that might take us as soon as I got back.

I told them my family would all be leaving too. I promised there would be no trace of us left. The Abramses would be gone from Germany as quickly as possible and would never return.'

Tilly and Aunt Hedy helped him into the flat and sat him in Opa's chair – which had had two of the legs kicked off during the pogrom. They had managed to pile up some of the water-damaged books that the German vandals had ruined in place of the missing legs, so it was still usable.

Mr Abrams groaned as he sat down. Wuffly sat next to him and he rested his hand on her head.

'What about Opa?' Oma asked, her voice quivering. '*What about Opa?* Is he coming home too?'

Mr Abrams put his head in his hands and wept.

'I couldn't help him,' he said. 'The things I've seen. My eyes will never forget the sight of evil, nor my ears forget the terrible things I've heard.'

So what Gretchen had said was really true, Tilly thought.

Oma used her apron to dab at the tears in her eyes.

'The Jews have been persecuted for hundreds of years, but still we survive,' Aunt Hedy said, squeezing Tilly's dad's shoulder. 'We'll survive this too.'

Oma was wringing her hands in her apron, over and over as if she was trying to squeeze away the truth that Opa wasn't coming home.

Wuffly looked from one of them to the other and whined softly.

'Remember the story of the Golem?' Aunt Hedy said, looking at Tilly.

Tilly nodded, but all she could think of was Hans's funny mudman Golem in the woods.

'Long long ago, it protected the Jews,' Aunt Hedy went on. 'There was one rule, though . . .'

'That the Golem must never work on the Sabbath, when all work is forbidden?' Tilly said absent-mindedly. She was wondering what Hans had done with the ceremonial *shofar* horn. The ear-splitting, eerie sound of it was said to have miraculously toppled the walls of Jericho, even longer ago than the Golem story. Was the *shofar* Hans had rescued now hidden in the woods with the Golem?

'One Sabbath the rabbi forgot to take the rolled-up parchment from the Golem's mouth, and the Golem became an abomination,' Mr Abrams said, his voice sounding like it was coming from far away. 'It was raging and out of control . . .'

'Like Hitler and his men,' Oma said, and her voice cracked as the tears flowed down her face.

Tilly shook her head because she thought Hitler was a lot worse. The Golem couldn't help himself but the *Führer* could.

'It killed many people, both Jew and Gentile, before the rabbi was finally able to pull the rolled parchment from its mouth. Once that was done the creature stopped and became as lifeless as clay from the riverbank. But the rabbi, terrified of what had happened, hid the creature away in the attic of the synagogue – where some say it still remains to this day.'

'We could do with finding that Golem to help us now,' Tilly said.

'We could indeed,' Aunt Hedy agreed. 'Now do you see why you have to go to England?' She told Mr Abrams about Tilly's refusal to leave. 'It's lucky I put her name on the *Kindertransport* list.'

'If you get a place, you must go, Tilly. You have to,' her father said. 'I want you to live a life where you don't have to be frightened of being beaten, or worse; of having your beautiful hair cut by thugs, or worse; of you and the people you love being put in prison camps, *or worse . . .*'

'All right, I'll go,' Tilly said, although she really didn't want to leave her family. Especially now that they needed her more than ever.

Aunt Hedy sighed with relief.

'And I'll join you as soon as I can,' said her father, clasping her hand.

'So long as I can take Wuffly with me,' Tilly added. It would be much easier going to a new country, a country whose language she didn't even speak, if she had her dog with her too.

Aunt Hedy looked horrified. 'Of course you can't take Wuffly! What on earth are you thinking? You can't even take more than one small suitcase.'

'Wuffly's very small,' Tilly said. She'd probably fit in a small bag or suitcase. Only for short while, of course – otherwise that would be cruel. And Wuffly wouldn't put up with it for long!

Aunt Hedy shook her head. 'If any of the children selected to go on the *Kindertransport* disobey the rules, then the train will stop and there will be terrible consequences both for them and for anyone else trying to help them. You could prevent children from escaping, Tilly. Do you want to ruin everything for the others? Do you want to put them in danger? Do you want to send them to the concentration camps?'

Tilly shook her head because of course she didn't, although her heart would break if Wuffly stayed behind without her. Her family could be arrested at any time. What would Wuffly do then? She loved her so much, and more than anything she wanted the little dog to be safe. But Tilly wasn't sure she had a choice any more.

Chapter 17

'You're going tomorrow, Tilly,' Aunt Hedy said when she came back from the community centre a few weeks later. 'There's a train leaving from Hamburg Station tomorrow at midnight.'

'So soon?' Tilly gasped.

'Not soon enough,' said Aunt Hedy. 'Everyone would like to have the opportunity you have. Germany's not safe for Jewish people. Not safe for anyone with *you know who* in charge.'

She now didn't even dare say Hitler's name in case someone heard her through the thin walls of the flat and reported them.

'I need to take Wuffly to Gretchen – she'll be safe there,' Tilly said. She hadn't seen or spoken to Gretchen since she'd come to Grindel and told them about Opa. But Tilly knew Gretchen loved Wuffly and would take care of her. Even if Gretchen didn't want to be friends any more after what had been said, she wouldn't turn her back on the little dog. Or, at least, Tilly didn't think she would.

Very early the next morning, Wuffly hurried excitedly after Tilly as she went down the stairs. The little dachshund loved going for walks, even ones in icy-cold weather when it was only just getting light and the person you were with strode very fast.

Tilly was dreading the meeting with Gretchen's mother. She knew she wouldn't be at all pleased to see her and Wuffly, but it was the safest place for Wuffly to be. She couldn't stay with Dad and Aunt Hedy and Oma because it was too dangerous – her family could be taken by the *Gestapo* at any time. What would happen to Wuffly then?

Gretchen lived near Neuengamme, where Tilly's family had once lived, but all the houses were now decorated with Nazi flags. Many of the front gates also had signs on them saying No Jews.

Tilly shuddered at the sight, but she wanted Wuffly to be safe, and Wuffly *would* be safe here with Gretchen.

When they reached Gretchen's house, number 23, she found they too had a No Jews sign outside. Tilly sighed, but she wasn't really that surprised. She ignored it, opened the gate, walked up the path and rapped on the door using the metal knocker in the shape of an eagle.

Gretchen's brother, Fritz, opened it and frowned when he saw Tilly and Wuffly.

'You shouldn't be here,' he said, looking up and down the street. 'What do you want?'

Wuffly gave a wag of her tail, but Fritz didn't stroke her.

'I'm going to England,' Tilly said as she picked Wuffly up. The little dog gave her face a lick. 'And I need Gretchen to look after Wuffly while I'm gone.'

Fritz took Wuffly from Tilly.

'Will you look after her?' Tilly asked. 'She'll be safe here.'

'Yes,' said Fritz, 'but only on one condition.'

'What's that?'

'That you never come back here and you don't contact my sister again.'

Tilly gasped. If she agreed to Fritz's condition, then she would never be able to make up with Gretchen.

But Wuffly would be safe here, safer than anywhere else she could think of. And that was the most important thing to her.

Tilly nodded.

'You agree?'

'Yes.'

'Then swear it.'

'I swear.'

Wuffly wriggled in Fritz's arms and looked over at Tilly.

Tilly stretched out her hand to give Wuffly one last goodbye stroke, but Fritz shut the door with his foot.

Tilly stared at the closed door as tears ran down her face. It was so hard walking away from Wuffly after she'd promised never to leave her. Tilly couldn't bear it. She turned and ran back up the path and out of the gate.

'What's Wuffly doing here again?' Gretchen said sleepily, coming down the stairs from her room, still in her pyjamas. 'Hey, Wuffly.' She patted her legs as Fritz put Wuffly down and the little dog ran over to her for a stroke.

'Where's Tilly?' Gretchen asked Fritz.

He pulled an odd sort of face that she couldn't quite work out.

'What is it?' she asked.

'The Jewish girl doesn't want to be in touch any more . . .'

'Oh,' Gretchen replied sadly.

'She's going to England and she's left you her dog to look after,' Fritz told her.

'England! Why's she going to England?' Gretchen didn't understand. She and Wuffly padded into the kitchen.

'She's probably on the midnight *Kindertransport* train leaving tonight,' said Gretchen's dad, who was eating his breakfast and had overheard the conversation.

'I've got to say goodbye!' Gretchen said.

'No!' said her mother.

'Eat your breakfast,' her father told her. 'I'll walk with you to school today.'

Later, after Gretchen had left for school with her father, Mrs Schmidt went upstairs to open the window and air her daughter's bedroom. She was utterly livid to find Wuffly lying on Gretchen's bed.

'Get off there, you dirty dog!' she shouted.

Wuffly immediately jumped off the bed, her tail between her legs. She wasn't exactly sure what she'd done wrong, but she knew it must have been something very bad.

'Out, out!' Mrs Schmidt continued shouting. 'Out of this room, out of this house!'

Wuffly ran down the stairs and into the kitchen as fast as she could, closely followed by Gretchen's mother. Mrs Schmidt opened the back door, shooed Wuffly outside and then slammed it after her. 'Good riddance! Bad dog.'

Wuffly waited patiently to be let back in and forgiven, but the door didn't open and it started to spit with rain instead. She whined and scratched at the door but still no one opened it. The rain was getting heavier. The little dog was soaked through by the time she decided to turn and head off into the woodland beyond the garden.

Here there were so many tantalizing, interesting smells for her sensitive nose to investigate. Smells that were even stronger and fresher when the rain eventually stopped.

The wild boar piglets Wuffly and Tilly had seen before came out of their nest to sniff at Wuffly, but the mother boar called them back with a shrill cry. Then she too sniffed at the intruder, and once she'd grunted her approval the piglets were allowed back.

When they'd all said hello to the dachshund, the little ones headed to the stream for a cool drink, only to find a fox had beaten them to it.

Wuffly wagged her tail and the fox trotted over to her. Then when Wuffly had had her drink, the two of them played in the meadow close to the barbed wire and the camp beyond it.

The German Shepherd guard dog on the other side of the fence came running over to them, barking and wagging its tail, wanting to play too.

'*Was ist das?*' the soldier on patrol shouted, running over to where the dog was barking. He held up his rifle and other soldiers came running from all directions, also shouting.

The fox heard them and scampered away, so Wuffly ran after it.

The soldiers looked through the fence, trying to see what the German Shepherd had seen.

'Was it a spy?' they asked each other.

The German Shepherd gave a whine and sat down, looking in the direction that Wuffly and the fox had gone.

The dog handler gazed at her and shook his head. 'Probably some wild animal she wanted to play with out there,' he said. 'She's been taught to react differently, to attack, if it's a person,' he added.

'Still, we'd better check it out,' a second soldier said.

'Could be anything,' said a third.

'Let's go.'

The soldiers made their way to the massive padlocked gates with the German Shepherd in tow.

Wuffly was still in the woodland, but the fox had run off to its den and didn't come out again. She looked through the wire fence once the shouting had stopped, hoping the German Shepherd would come over to play.

Soon she heard the sound of soldiers yelling in the woods behind her. Their rifles were at the ready. The German Shepherd was with them and strained and panted on its lead.

Wuffly looked up and wagged her tail as a boy came running through the trees and scooped her up.

'A dog!' one of the soldiers said.

'I saw a dog!'

'Where?'

'Just ahead, but I can't see it now.'

'Maybe it's lost.'

'Maybe it was a fox.'

'No . . . I don't think so . . .'

Wuffly looked up at Hans She'd met him before, down at the stream with Tilly. She gave his face a quick lick. She very much liked this boy.

Hans waited until he was sure the soldiers and their dog had gone. Then he carried Wuffly with him to his hidden camp in the woods. It wasn't far from the stream and Wuffly's tummy was soon full of delicious freshly-caught fish.

After she'd eaten her fill, she curled up on a bed of crisp brown leaves in the winter sunshine for an afternoon nap.

'Wuffly, Wuffly!' a voice cried in the distance and Wuffly's ears pricked up. She looked at the boy, who was sketching in his book. Hans didn't talk to her like Tilly and other people did, but Wuffly could understand him just as well through his body language. And she trusted him.

'Wuffly!'

The dog gave a little whine, but the boy still didn't look up.

'Wuffly – where are you?'

Wuffly jumped up and ran a little way towards the voice. Then she stopped and looked back at Hans.

Hans glanced at Wuffly with a frown on his face. He closed the book, stuck his pencil behind his ear and followed her.

Wuffly kept on running and stopping, running and stopping, until the voice was really quite loud and only just ahead. Still the boy didn't seem to hear it.

'Wuffly!' Gretchen cried when she saw her. 'Oh, Wuffly, I've been looking everywhere. I'm so pleased I found you.'

She knelt down and Wuffly ran to her, to be stroked and stroked.

The little dog looked over at Hans, who was now crouched low, hidden by the ferns. Gretchen didn't see him and the boy kept very still.

'Let's get you home and give you something nice to eat,' Gretchen said. 'You must be so hungry. I bet you were scared out here, lost and all alone.'

Wuffly stared in the direction of Hans and gave a whine, but he didn't come out. As Wuffly and Gretchen made their way home, Hans followed them, unseen, from a distance.

Gretchen wasn't sure if her mum had something to do with Wuffly being out in the woods alone, or if Wuffly had escaped in an attempt to find Tilly. But when they got back to her house, Gretchen's mum was out, so Wuffly could come inside and both Gretchen and the dog were glad about that.

'Now let's see what tasty thing we can find for you to eat,' Gretchen said.

Wuffly thought this was a good idea and wagged her tail.

The first thing Gretchen found in the cool cupboard were the leftovers of the beef stew, or *sauerbraten*, from the previous night.

Wuffly thought the stew was very fine indeed. She licked her lips when she'd finished the small bowlful that Gretchen gave her, followed by a long drink of cool water.

Chapter 18

The hours before Tilly had to leave were gone in no time at all. She packed a change of clothes and took the photo of her mum, and a photo of Wuffly as a puppy.

'I love you, Oma,' she said, kissing the old lady's wrinkly cheek. She didn't know when or if she'd see her grandmother again.

Oma didn't reply. She didn't even seem to know who Tilly was any more.

Tilly squeezed her grandmother's hand as a tear ran down her face. She'd cried so much today that her eyes felt gritty and sore.

'Ready?' said Tilly's father. Tilly nodded.

'We have to hurry,' Aunt Hedy told them as Mr Abrams took his battered hat from the broken hatstand.

'Will Oma be OK?' Tilly asked, but neither her father or Aunt Hedy answered.

'Let's go.'

They hurried out into the night to the train station. On the way they saw other families with children heading that way too.

'Why do we have to leave so late?' Tilly asked her aunt.

'Because the German government doesn't want the world press to know what's happening,' Aunt Hedy told her. 'There was enough bad publicity after the pogrom. They don't want to make it worse.'

They went past the hateful Nazi swastika flags and stone lions that guarded the entrance to the station. Inside, it was packed to bursting with children and their relatives. People were milling about, their faces and voices strained. Their hopeful words didn't match the way their eyes looked.

The steam train was already waiting on the platform. The station was so noisy with everyone talking and jostling that Tilly, her father and aunt could barely hear each other speak.

'Write as soon as you get there to let us know,' Aunt Hedy shouted.

'And hopefully we'll be able to join you soon in England,' her father said.

Tilly looked at Aunt Hedy. Her aunt was about to disagree. Tilly knew she wanted to go to Palestine rather than England. 'It's OK,' she mouthed and Aunt Hedy nodded.

Tilly hugged her father and then her aunt, who squeezed her really tightly.

'Stay strong,' Aunt Hedy told her. 'Stay strong!'

Tilly looked up and frowned, thinking she'd seen a familiar face. 'Hans!' she called out, but then remembered he couldn't hear her.

She pushed through the crowds to reach him. Her father and Aunt Hedy followed.

'You going on the train?' she signed to him. Was Hans coming to England too?

Hans shook his head. 'No, I'll stay here and help people,' he signed back.

Tilly shook her head. How was he going to do that? She made the sign for 'dangerous'.

Hans shook his head again, grinned and pulled a small round piece of baked clay from his pocket. It had tiny pieces of clear glass for its eyes, nose and mouth. He handed it to her.

Tilly's mouth fell open as she stared at the little figure, her eyes filled with tears. It was such a kind and unexpected gift.

'Thank you,' she signed.

Hans gave a nod. 'GOLEM,' he spelt with his fingers. 'Protect.'

Tilly's father shook Hans's hand. They'd met before when they'd lived at the old house.

Aunt Hedy didn't know Hans, but she gave him a little nervous wave.

'*Children to the edge of the platform. Proceed to the train,*' the voice over the tannoy said. Hans disappeared into the crowds of people.

'You have to go now, Tilly,' Aunt Hedy said.

'Be safe, my darling,' said Mr Abrams. 'I'll join you as soon as I can.'

'I love you Papa, and you, Aunt Hedy, even if you are a *lobbus* sometimes,' Tilly told them.

Aunt Hedy chuckled even though tears were running down her face.

'I'll miss you,' she said.

'*Parents and guardians, make your way off the platform,*' the voice over the loudspeaker said.

Soldiers with guns approached to make sure the orders were obeyed.

The doors to the train were opened and Tilly joined the other children as they boarded. She touched the mini Golem in her pocket and looked into the crowd to see if she could spot Hans, but she couldn't catch sight of him anywhere. She wondered how he knew she would be at the station, or if it had just been a coincidence. There wasn't time to think about it now.

It was after eleven thirty when Gretchen and Wuffly sneaked from the house. Fritz was out and her mother had finally fallen asleep listening to the radio.

Gretchen took her bicycle from the porch, put Wuffly in the basket and cycled as fast as she could to the station. She was determined to say goodbye to Tilly before she left.

But at the station there were hundreds of families crowding the concourse saying goodbye. So many people there was barely room to breathe.

Gretchen bit her bottom lip. How was she supposed to find Tilly among all these crowds of jostling men, women and children?

Wuffly crouched close to Gretchen away from the many feet moving about. Most of the people were too distracted, excited and upset to look where they were going. She gave a yelp as someone stepped on her. Gretchen picked the little dog up so she wouldn't get trodden on again.

'It's OK, Wuffly. We're going to find Tilly to say goodbye,' Gretchen told her.

Just then, Wuffly saw Hans and tried to jump out of her arms.

'No, Wuffly!' Gretchen said.

Wuffly looked at Hans and gave a whine.

There! There was Tilly, her father and aunt. Gretchen pushed her way through the crowd as they made their way towards the waiting train. *'Entschuldige! Entschuldigen Sie!'*

Parents were being told to leave their children, but Gretchen and Wuffly ran on to the platform after Tilly and saw her go up the steps into the train.

'Tilly!' Gretchen yelled, trying to push her way past people who didn't want to move. 'Tilly!'

Wuffly jumped out of Gretchen's arms and barked and barked as she ran.

Tilly heard the barks.

'Wuffly?' she said, turning and trying to shove past the throngs of children that were clambering on board behind her.

She reached the door and saw the little dog on the platform.

'Wuffly!'

'On board!' a soldier told Tilly, pushing her back on to the train before she could get down the steps. He closed the door and locked it from the outside.

Tilly was squashed on to the train with hundreds of other children, some nervous older Jewish teenagers, grown-up chaperones and bullying Nazi soldiers.

'*Wuffly!*' Tilly screamed.

But it was too late. The whistle sounded and the train started pulling out of the station.

Then suddenly, other shrill, urgent whistles were blown repeatedly.

The train stopped.

Tilly looked out of the window as she tried to push her way past the other children again.

A father had pulled his little boy out of the train window, unable to bear the thought of him going to England after all. Once the little boy was safely in his father's arms and not half in and half out of the window, the whistle blew again and the train left the station.

'Back into the compartments!' a soldier with a gun ordered. 'Get back now!'

Wuffly was waiting at the train door that Tilly had gone into. Her tail was wagging – she'd found Tilly at last. She barked to tell Tilly to open it and take her too, not to leave her behind. She barked and barked again as the train pulled out of the station.

'Wuffly!' Gretchen called as she ran down the platform after the little dog. She didn't want her to be crushed by the train's huge wheels.

Wuffly ran along the platform until there was no more platform left, and then she ran down on to the tracks and along the wooden slats between the rails as the train picked up speed and thundered away into the moonlit night.

'Wuffly!' Gretchen called, but she didn't run after the little dog once the train had left the station. Ever since she was a small girl her father had warned her against stepping on the tracks.

'Wuffly,' she called, bewildered and despairing. 'Wuffly!' Tears streamed down her face as she stared after the train with her best friend on board and the little dog running after it. Now she'd lost them both.

As the train disappeared into the dark night, Wuffly came to a stop, lifted up her head and howled.

The train didn't return and nor did Tilly. Wuffly walked on and on until her paws were sore. Eventually she could walk no further and she lay down on the railway tracks, exhausted.

Chapter 19

Tilly's compartment contained seven other children, from the youngest who was only four years old and sucked her thumb almost continuously, to the eldest, who was thirteen-year-old Tilly.

'Don't worry,' Tilly told the other children, swallowing hard as she thought of Wuffly being left behind. 'We are going on a wonderful journey.'

None of the children had been to England or knew any English, so Tilly taught them the few words that she knew: *Hello*, *Goodbye*, *Please* and *Thank you*.

'I'm Horst. Do you know any jokes?' one of the boys asked her.

Tilly nodded. 'Can a kangaroo jump higher than a house?' she asked.

Horst's face wrinkled in thought and then his eyes opened wide as he got the answer. 'Yes! Because a house can't jump!'

Tilly grinned and nodded.

She soon discovered that some of the children on board the train had been on it for a lot longer than she had. Hamburg was one of the last stops on this trip.

'Berlin?' she asked, looking at the label round the neck of the little girl sitting opposite, sucking her thumb and holding a soft toy dog with floppy ears. The child nodded.

'And what's your dog's name?'

'Jodie.'

'I have a dog,' Tilly said, and her heart ached as she thought about Wuffly's little face looking up at the train, wanting to come on board. In her head she could still hear the dachshund barking. 'She's called Wuffly because she likes to wuff.'

The little girl gave a half smile.

'My name's Lotte.'

'I'm Tilly.'

Lotte looked very, very tired.

Other children held on to toys they had brought with them. Josepha had a doll wearing a striped knitted dress.

They hadn't been going for long when the train came to a juddering halt. Out of the window Tilly saw more soldiers getting on board.

'What's happening?' the children asked Tilly in a panic.

'Are we going home now?' Lotte asked hopefully. 'I want to see my mummy.'

'Just stay calm, everything will be fine,' Tilly told the other children, although she really didn't know if it would be or not.

She heard the sound of heavy boots coming down the corridor. Children started crying. The door of the next carriage to theirs opened and a soldier began to shout.

The next moment, Tilly's carriage door opened and two black-booted soldiers, one of them wearing the SS insignia, came in. Tilly saw Horst's face turn white with fear. He began to shake uncontrollably and even his teeth were chattering.

'Good morning,' Tilly said to the soldiers. Her voice only shook a little bit. It *was* morning, just . . . a little before one o'clock. But she needn't have bothered because they just ignored her.

The SS soldier pointed to a small suitcase on the floor. There wasn't enough room for all of the luggage to fit above the seats.

'Open.'

Nobody moved and the suitcase remained closed.

'Open!' the soldier commanded.

It wasn't Tilly's suitcase, but the rest of the children just sat frozen with fear, so Tilly opened it and lifted the lid.

Once she'd done so, the other soldier picked up the open suitcase and dumped everything inside it on the floor.

'Open!' the SS soldier said, pointing to each of the suitcases in the luggage rack above their seats.

Tilly got each of them down and opened them.

Inside the suitcases there were clothes, toothbrushes, combs and toys. Nothing of any real interest for the Nazi soldiers as far as Tilly could see. It wasn't like the children's bags had gold or hidden treasure inside them.

She bit her bottom lip as the contents of all the suitcases were tipped out. Soon there was a pitiful pile of belongings on the floor between the two bench seats that the frightened children were sitting on.

'My dog,' said Lotte, when she saw the soldiers looking at her. She clenched her toy against her chest. 'Don't hurt Jodie.'

The soldier snatched the dog from her hands and stamped on it, and then ground his booted foot into its face while the other soldier laughed as if it was the funniest thing he'd ever seen. Tilly pressed her lips together. She knew it would only make it worse if she said anything. Lotte went to grab her toy, but Tilly quickly took hold of the child's hand and shook her head.

Lotte wiped at the tears running down her face. Her hands left dirty streaks across her pale cheeks.

The soldiers moved on to the next compartment where Tilly could hear the soldier with the SS insignia shouting, 'Open.'

The other children in Tilly's compartment looked at the pile of their belongings on the floor and then back at Tilly. They didn't know if they were allowed to put them back in their suitcases and nor did she. The soldiers might come back and be angry with them if they did so without asking for permission.

'Wait,' she said, and they did. They waited and waited but the soldiers didn't come back. Tilly could hear them moving down the corridor opening doors. She heard someone scream. Saw a violin being thrown from a window. No one in Tilly's compartment spoke.

Tilly touched the tiny Golem in her pocket that Hans had given her. It brought some comfort even though it was only made from clay.

Lotte picked up Jodie and hugged her.

'The bad man hurt her,' she said as she gave Jodie to Tilly to check over.

Tilly dusted the dirt from the man's boot off the toy. One of its button eyes was missing.

'You'll need to take extra special care of Jodie,' Tilly told her. 'She'll want lots of hugs and a new button for her eye.'

Lotte nodded solemnly and took Jodie back from her. 'Tell us a story,' she said, squeezing herself into the space next to Tilly.

Tilly looked at the other children who were all nodding, and who looked very tired.

'All right,' she said. 'This is the story of Wuffly, the bravest dog in the world.' She wished more than anything that Wuffly could be here too. But then she remembered the cruelty of the soldiers and thought it best that she wasn't.

'What sort of dog?' Horst asked.

'A black-and-tan dachshund,' Tilly told him.

'Don't make anything bad happen,' Lotte said fearfully.

Tilly nodded.

'This story happened a long, long time ago in the land of fairy stories far, far away, where unicorns sing and elephants love to eat apples and little Wuffly looked after them all . . .'

Lotte snuggled up to Jodie with her thumb in her mouth and fell asleep. Soon all the children were sleeping.

Tilly looked out of the window and watched as the moonlit countryside raced past. Her last thought before she too fell asleep was of Wuffly barking. The little dog would think she didn't want her and had left her behind at the station on purpose, when that wasn't true at all.

Tilly wanted her pet so badly it made her heart ache. She wanted to go back to the days when she woke up to find Wuffly lying on her bed. To the time when the little dog would roll over on to her back for a tummy rub. Most of all she wished her mum was still with them and that they lived at the old house with Oma and Opa coming to stay. She wished that she and Gretchen were still friends because she didn't have any friends now, except maybe for Hans. She missed Gretchen, missed her badly. If only she could have said goodbye before she left.

It was just getting light when the Nazi soldiers got off the train at the last station before the border between Holland and Germany.

A little while later, but still very early so most of the children, though not Tilly, were asleep, some ladies from Holand came on board. They had mugs of hot chocolate and buttered bread for the children.

'My name is Truus Wijsmuller and you're safe now,' a large lady told the children, waking the rest of them up as she came into their compartment. 'I'm one of the *Kindertransport* organizers.'

'I know about you,' said Horst, rubbing at his sleepy eyes. 'Children call you *Tante Truus*.'

'Yes, they do,' the lady smiled.

'We're safe, really safe, now?' Tilly said.

Truus nodded. 'Yes, you are.'

As the children sipped the hot chocolate and ate the food, they looked at each other as if they still couldn't quite believe it. Once everyone finally accepted that the bullying Nazi soldiers had really gone and weren't coming back, the sombre atmosphere of the train turned to one of pure joy.

'We're in Holland.'

'We're safe – we're really safe!'

The children started singing and dancing and laughing – they were all caught up in the relief and excitement of the moment.

Tilly joined in as Lotte danced round and round in circles with Jodie, her face beaming. Someone knew the English words to 'Jingle Bells' and everyone sang it as loudly as they could because it was snowing outside – although no one really understood what it meant.

'Thank you,' Tilly said to Truus. 'Thank you so much.'

'Make the most of your life, my dear,' Truus told her as the Dutch ladies left and the train set off again for the last part of the journey to the Hook of Holland. 'Make the most of every precious moment you have.'

'I will,' Tilly promised. 'I will.'

As they got off the train and boarded the giant boat for England, Tilly held Lotte's hand. She looked through the wooden slats of the gangplank at the water below them. Soon this would be English sea. Soon their journey would end.

The horn of the ferry blasted and made everyone jump. Then they were off, across the waves that crashed and swirled beneath them. Tilly looked back at the land they'd come from and thought about her family, Wuffly, Gretchen and Hans.

Chapter 20

In the woodlands close to Gretchen's house, Wuffly woke up next to her rescuer, Hans. He'd found her lying on the train tracks, gently picked her up and carried her home to his cave. She put her sore paw out to him and he stroked her. Wuffly knew by the soothing sounds he made that he was telling her everything was going to be OK.

It was getting light. Outside, the sun had streaked the winter sky with pink light. In the distance Wuffly heard the sound of a passing train.

Hans shared his breakfast fish with Wuffly and carried the little dog through the trees back to Gretchen's garden.

When they got there, Hans put the ceremonial *shofar* he'd saved from the flames to his lips and blew. A high blast came from it.

Wuffly looked up at Hans and wagged her tail. She liked the sound. So did Hans. He could feel it vibrating as he played.

Inside her room at the back of the house, Gretchen was finally asleep after a restless, worried night full of images of Tilly and lost little Wuffly. The haunting sound of the *shofar* crept into Gretchen's dreams and she opened her eyes, confused. She'd never heard anything like it.

She heard a similar sound again, this time, consisting of three sharp blass.

When Gretchen looked out of her window, all she saw was Wuffly sitting on the grass gazing up at her. Gretchen frowned and scratched her head. It didn't make sense. The little dog couldn't make a sound like the one she'd heard. It was more like a horn, or a trumpet. Nothing like a dog's bark. Then Gretchen grinned because she didn't really care – she was just so pleased to see Wuffly!

She raced down the stairs and out on to the wet grass, her bare feet soaked by the morning dew as she hugged Wuffly to her.

'I'm so glad you're OK,' she said over and over again. 'So, so glad.' She hadn't known if she'd ever see Wuffly again after the dog had run on to the train tracks last night. 'Let's go and find you something tasty to eat.'

Wuffly trotted beside Gretchen as she headed back into the house.

'Sausages?' Gretchen asked and Wuffly wagged her tail because sausages were always very fine indeed.

Once the little dachshund had eaten, Gretchen took her upstairs to her room. Wuffly jumped up on to the bed and watched while Gretchen put on her German Young Girls' League uniform and tied her neck scarf.

'Who's eaten all the sausages?' Mrs Schmidt shouted from downstairs.

'Sssh,' Gretchen whispered, putting her finger to her lips as she smiled at Wuffly.

'What's that dog doing in here?' Mrs Schmidt demanded, coming into Gretchen's room. 'I told you it wasn't allowed in the house. Now I know where those sausages went!'

'Oh, Mum, please. It's too cold for Wuffly outside,' Gretchen pleaded.

'Then shut it in the playhouse – or the shed.'

Gretchen really didn't want to shut Wuffly in the playhouse, but at least she'd be out of the wind there. She was also worried about the dog running off and getting lost again after last night.

'I'll be home soon,' Gretchen reassured Wuffly as she put her inside the playhouse and closed the door. She dropped a little bit of cheese through the window and the dachshund gobbled it up.

Gretchen took out her bicycle and rode to school. A tall man wearing black boots and an SS uniform was standing by the gates as she cycled into the playground and put her bicycle in the rack.

Everyone else at school was wearing their Hitler Youth uniforms too. Today was a special day. Members of the SS were coming to talk to the children, and the man wearing the long boots was one of them. He spoke to the whole school from the stage in the hall.

'We are pleased to announce that the nearby village of Neuengamme has been honoured to host a new camp at the old brick factory. At this camp, prisoners will be expected to work hard, under Aryan supervision, of course. You, my children, are those future supervisors and guards. You, Hitler's children, will enforce the *Führer*'s will.'

The children around Gretchen started clapping and cheering.

'As soon as you are old enough, there will be employment for all at Neuengamme. In the meantime, there will be a school trip so all of you can see how those that are not loyal to the *Führer* can expect to be treated.'

Around her, excited students signed up to go on the trip to see the new camp. Gretchen added her name to the list because she didn't want to draw any attention to herself, but even the idea of the new camp brought back terrible memories of Tilly's grandad.

'The prisoners' first job will be building the barracks where their guards will sleep, and then they will build more for themselves to rest in. It will be hard work and we will need guards of integrity and firmness to ensure they do not slack. Guards whom, hopefully, you yourselves may want to become once you are old enough.'

When no more cheese dropped from the sky, Wuffly jumped on to the small chair, squeezed out of the window and went running into the woods to find her friend.

Hans was by the stream when Wuffly arrived, her tail wagging. He'd made a net to catch fish. It was wedged in between rocks that he'd piled up on either side so the fish only had a narrow area to swim through and would easily get caught.

The little dog watched as Hans kept very still, watching the water and waiting for the telltale sign that a fish was close by. The glint of a fin beneath the surface in the winter sunshine was enough.

Hans liked to go fishing in the mornings because that was when the fish came out to eat and were most active. But Wuffly found it frustrating to wait for the net to catch the fishes and when she saw one heading towards her she jumped into the water and came back with it in her jaws.

Hans was amazed and excited. He grinned, waving his hands about.

Wuffly was very pleased that Hans was happy, and when she spotted another fish, she dived into the stream after that one too.

She didn't catch every fish that she went after, but she did get quite a few.

When Hans had cooked that day's catch on the small fire and they'd eaten them and cleared everything away, the boy picked up his notebook and a pencil that he'd sharpened with his penknife. Then they made their way through the trees to the guarded camp that Wuffly had found.

All seemed quiet and no one was patrolling the fence.

Hans crept closer and Wuffly followed him. This was the closest he'd dared to go. He paced the exact length of the perimeter and made a careful record of it in his notebook.

Suddenly a voice shouted. Wuffly looked up sharply and Hans saw what had alarmed her out of the corner of his eye.

The soldier with the German Shepherd was charging towards them.

Hans immediately started running and Wuffly ran after him. Together they raced back to the cave, jumping over roots and under tree branches, panting heavily.

Hans pulled the woven twigs and moss camouflage he'd made over the entrance to the cave. Now no one would know that they were there.

Inside the cave, he stroked the little dog and their breathing gradually calmed. His hand brushed against Wuffly's collar and the locket round her neck.

Hans took off Wuffly's red-and-gold collar and unclasped the locket. Then he carefully tore the sheet of paper with the drawing and measurements of the new camp on it from his notebook. He folded the sheet over and over until it was as small as it possibly could be. Then he put it inside the locket and closed it.

Wuffly stretched up her head for a stroke and Hans put the collar back on her. It was time to take the little dog back to Gretchen's garden. Hans pulled the camouflage away from the entrance to the cave and they set off cautiously.

When Gretchen got home from school, her father was in the garden over by the vegetable shed.

As she walked over to him she thought he didn't look well – there was a grey pallor to his skin and he had dark circles under his eyes.

'The little Houdini dog won't be able to escape from here once I've bought a lock for the door,' he said.

'What do you mean?' she asked.

'The little Jewish dog. Your mother saw it run off. Houdini the escape artist was Jewish too, you know.'

'Not again,' said Gretchen. 'Maybe Wuffly needs to go to the new prison.' But she was only joking and immediately realized it truly wasn't that funny. She didn't want Wuffly to go there. She didn't want anyone to go there.

Gretchen told her father about the new camp at Neuengamme.

'The SS said the children from my school could work there one day.'

Her dad looked horrified.

'No, Gretchen,' he said. 'You should *never* work there. If you had seen the things that I've seen . . . The things done with the blessing of the government. Things a man shouldn't do to another man – or woman. People locked in the trains pass little pieces of folded paper to me through the narrow gaps. *Let my children know I love them*, they whisper. *Please pass this on, I didn't have a chance to say goodbye.* And what can I do but take their messages – until the soldiers see and order me to throw them away.' Her dad's voice broke on the last word.

'It's OK, Dad. I'll never work at the camp,' Gretchen said.

'But don't let anyone besides me hear you say so,' her father warned, looking just as worried as before. 'To everyone else you are a loyal Hitler girl and must always appear to be so.'

Tears started to run down her father's face.

'Dad, Dad! It's OK,' Gretchen said. 'I won't put us in any danger.'

'Once you say yes, you can't say no and they'll want you to do more and more.'

'More what?' Gretchen asked.

'First it was take the Polish Jews to no-man's-land during *Polenaktion*, then the *Kristallnacht* prisoners . . .'

Gretchen nodded. That trip was seared into her memory.

'But now I am expected to take people almost every day. Only now I know, *I know* how the prisoners are treated. I see and I know, and *it's not right*. But it's too late for me to stop. I must keep driving people into hell and then one day, I am sure, someone will drive me there too. They couldn't take so many people without the railway. They're building more tracks right up to the camp gates.'

'Oh, Dad. You're just doing your job,' Gretchen said feebly.

'Be careful, Gretchen,' he said. 'Listen to me – you don't want to go there. *You don't want to see.*'

'Go where? See what?'

'Train drivers like me aren't allowed inside, but we hear and we see and sometimes we smell.' Gretchen didn't quite understand what her father meant, but it sounded so scary she didn't want to know.

'Then say you won't drive those trains,' Gretchen said. 'Say you'll do other routes.'

Her father shook his head. 'I don't have a choice,' he said finally as he stepped out of the shed. 'We'd better look for your missing dog.'

But when they went out into the garden, Wuffly was already sitting there, patiently waiting for them.

Chapter 21

Tilly held Lotte's hand and Lotte clasped Jodie, her toy dog, tightly when the ferry docked at Harwich and everyone had to get off.

Lotte had been very seasick on the way, as had many of the other children, but Tilly hadn't.

'The English Channel is notoriously rough,' one of the chaperones told Tilly as she went to the assistance of the other queasy children. 'I can't think why anyone would try and swim it for fun, but every year people do.'

Tilly shook her head. She couldn't imagine why anyone would risk trying to swim such a long way in such rough water. The only reason she could think of would be if they were truly, truly desperate.

Once they had landed in England, the Jewish chaperones from Germany, as well as the older Jewish teenagers who'd helped to look after the youngest ones and the babies had to get back on the ship and go home. Only children up to the age of seventeen were allowed to stay.

Tilly watched as they climbed the gangplank, on their way home to face who knew what.

Some of the *Kindertransport* children were staying at a nearby holiday camp called Dovercourt. They were taken away in a double-decker bus the colour of blood. But others, including Lotte, whose oma lived in Finchley, North London, were going on the train to the capital.

Tilly went on the train too and did her best to clean the little girl up on the way. The poor child had been sick down her coat, but luckily none had landed on Jodie.

Tilly wondered how her own oma was doing back at home. The last time she'd seen her she'd been lying on the mattress in Oma and Opa's old bedroom. Her hands had looked so frail and thin.

At London's Liverpool Street Station people from synagogues and churches, as well as relatives and friends and kind strangers, were there to pick the children up and take them away to start their new lives.

Most of the children had been told their parents would be joining them soon, so lots of them thought they were going on holiday. Tilly wanted to believe that too, very much, but she wasn't convinced.

'Oma!' Lotte cried with delight when she saw her grandmother. She hugged Tilly goodbye and asked her to stroke Jodie too. 'She likes you.'

'And I like her,' Tilly smiled.

Lotte waved as she and Jodie left the station with her oma.

'Mathilde Abrams, Mathilde Abrams!' a voice called and Tilly jumped up and headed over to one of the administration desks.

The lady smiled as she ticked off Tilly's name. A man wearing a uniform was standing next to the table. Tilly looked at him nervously. Above his pocket it said RSPCA. Was RSPCA the British version of the SS? A boy around her own age was standing next to the man. He didn't have a uniform on. He smiled and waved at her and Tilly half-smiled back, although she felt very nervous.

The man said something to her in English, but Tilly couldn't understand what it was. She shook her head.

The man didn't seem to mind. He pointed to his chest and said 'George Ward.'

'George Ward,' Tilly repeated, pointing at him.

The boy smiled and pointed to himself. 'Michael.'

'Michael,' said Tilly. Then she pointed to herself and said, 'Tilly.'

Michael and George repeated her name. Then George beckoned to her and Tilly followed him and Michael out of the station. George stopped at a van with the letters RSPCA on it and opened the door.

Tilly eyes felt scratchy and sore from tiredness as she got into the vehicle. *I'll just close my eyes for a moment*, she thought as they drove past more red buses. But in the next moment she was fast asleep.

Chapter 22

George Ward stopped the van outside number 39, a house at the end of a terrace of red brick houses that all looked the same.

Michael looked over at Tilly. 'She's sleeping, Dad. Should I wake her up?' he asked.

'Yes, but do it gently. You don't want to scare her and we don't know what horrors she's been through where she's come from.'

'Tilly,' Michael said softly; then a bit louder, 'Tilly.' But the girl continued to sleep.

Then the front door of number 39 opened and a large woman, with short curly brown hair, came down the path. She was wearing a long apron over her dress and slippers on her feet, and she was followed by three excited dogs and a curious cat.

Tilly had been dreaming about Wuffly and opened her eyes at the sound of barking.

'Wuffly?'

She looked at Michael and remembered where she was. Wuffly wasn't here.

The lady opened the van door and beamed at Tilly.

'Hello, there!' she said. Tilly knew that word.

'Hello,' said Tilly.

'Come on in,' the lady said, beckoning to Tilly. She got out of the van and was immediately surrounded by the dogs wagging their tails.

Tilly laughed as she crouched down and gave them each a stroke. She was glad her foster family had pets.

Michael looked at his dad and held up his thumbs. For Tilly to be happy here, she needed to be an animal lover and it looked like she was.

Tilly stopped to pet the cat as well before following her new family inside the house.

'She can't speak much English, Mum,' Michael said.

'Well, she'll soon learn if we all help her,' he was told.

An elderly yellow Labrador was waiting for them in the hallway.

'Meet Heggerty, our official meeter and greeter,' grinned Mrs Ward as Tilly knelt down to stroke the dog, whose thick tail was wagging like a pendulum. 'She's not as young as she used to be, but she's just as friendly,' Mrs Ward added.

'Mum, she can't understand you,' Michael said.

But Mrs Ward didn't care. 'Well, I can't just not say anything, can I? It'd be rude.'

Then it occurred to her that Tilly might need to use the toilet. She bet no one had asked her that. Mrs Ward touched Tilly on the shoulder and beckoned to her. Tilly followed her outside, past the chickens and a baby goat to the outhouse.

'Thank you,' Tilly said when she saw where they were going.

'Toilet,' Mrs Ward said.

That would have been a very useful English word to have learnt, but Tilly grinned because it was almost the same in German as English.

'*Toilette!*' she said, and headed inside and closed the door. High up in the corner of the ceiling Tilly saw a big spider lurking. 'I'm not scared of you any more,' she said. She didn't think she'd ever be frightened of spiders again. 'I can face anything now.'

*

When they came back inside, Mrs Ward smiled and pointed to Tilly's suitcase, which Tilly picked up. She followed the smiling lady up the stairs to a room with a closed door.

'Your room,' Mrs Ward said.

But as soon as Mrs Ward opened the door, a soaking black-and-white collie with bright blue eyes came racing out and leapt at Tilly in excitement, almost knocking her over.

143

'No!' Mrs Ward cried as Tilly laughed, even though she was all wet now. 'I shut her in your room because she's only a puppy and can cause havoc in two seconds flat,' Mrs Ward said, sighing heavily.

Tilly shook her head because she didn't understand a word of what Mrs Ward was saying – but she had a lively puppy licking her face.

Mrs Ward pointed to the black-and-white collie and said, 'Skye.'

'Skye,' Tilly repeated as she stood up and followed her into the room.

Mrs Ward had left a pair of Michael's pyjamas and a spare dressing gown of her own, which she now saw would be too big for the slight girl, on the bed for Tilly. There was a little jar of flowers on the bedside cabinet, which fortunately the puppy hadn't knocked over.

She'd also poured hot water into a shallow tin bath that she'd set on the rug. It was meant for Tilly to soothe her weary limbs in, but Skye had obviously assumed the bath was meant for her and made the most of it. Now the collie evidently thought it was time for a second dip and leapt in eagerly.

Mrs Ward and Tilly burst out laughing. Then Mrs Ward held up a towel and soap and pointed to Tilly to indicate that the bath had been meant for her.

Even though she couldn't speak the language, Tilly understood.

Mrs Ward went out and soon returned with two fresh pans of hot water to pour into the tin bath.

'Thank you,' Tilly said.

The puppy was looking very excited about the new water being poured into the bath, so Mrs Ward escorted Skye out to give Tilly some privacy.

Once Mrs Ward had closed the door, Tilly looked around her new room.

She took her coat off and removed the small Golem from the pocket. 'You brought me luck and helped me to feel brave,' she whispered as she set it on the bedside table.

She also took out Wuffly's broken name tag that she'd picked up off the ground on *Kristallnacht* and put it next to the Golem. The photo of her mum and the one of Wuffly were placed next to it. She thought her mum would have liked Mrs Ward very much.

Next she unpacked her few clothes and put them in the drawer.

Then she stepped into the bath. The warm water felt so relaxing it was all she could do not to fall asleep again. But she made sure she didn't because the Wards were waiting for her downstairs.

After that, she cleaned her teeth, put on the clothes that were on the bed, brushed her short hair and went back downstairs to join the Wards and their pets.

A miniature poodle, a black-and-brown King Charles Spaniel and a German Shepherd were lying on a rug by the hearth. There were lots of cats of different breeds sitting on shelves, chairs and the windowsill. There were birdcages containing canaries and budgies and even two guinea pigs in a large cage in the corner.

Mrs Ward smiled and patted the sofa, on which were several cushions embroidered with cats and dogs. Tilly went to sit next to her. Heggerty climbed up on the other side, snuggling in closely as Tilly gave her a stroke.

While Tilly had been having her bath, Michael had been busy writing English words on bits of paper and then sticking them around the living room and kitchen. He'd stuck them on everything he could think of. Even the stand on which the cockatoo perched.

'*Cupboard, carpet, door, sofa* . . .' Tilly read.

'Tea, dear?' Mrs Ward asked her. There were more labels on the teapot and cups and saucers and sugar bowl. Tilly had already had her first sip of tea on the ship coming over and she didn't really like it much. But Mrs Ward was smiling and nodding as if she thought the horrible brown water in the teapot was the most delicious thing in the world.

Tilly smiled back and Mrs Ward poured some into a cup for her and added milk.

'Sugar?' Mrs Ward said, indicating the china pot with sugar lumps in it. Mrs Ward added two cubes to her own tea and gave it a stir.

Tilly thought sugar couldn't make the tea any worse. She added two lumps and took a sip. Definitely better now than the tea they'd been given on the ship. She added two more sugar lumps and it was better still.

Mrs Ward beamed.

'Cake?' Even that had a label next to it.

'Thank you,' said Tilly.

Heggerty drifted off to sleep and began to snore softly. Skye came running in and started pulling at the tie of Tilly's dressing gown.

Tilly smiled as she stroked the puppy. She loved being around so many pets.

'You like animals?' Michael asked her, pointing at Skye and smiling.

Tilly nodded.

'You have a dog?' Michael asked her, pointing to Skye and drawing a little question mark in the air.

Tilly nodded and then she remembered the photo of her and Wuffly. She ran upstairs to fetch it.

'Wuffly,' she said, giving the photograph to Michael when she came back downstairs. She crossed her arms over her heart to show the sign for 'love'.

'Wuffly,' Michael said, looking at the little dog's picture. He made the sign for 'love' too. But then he added the British sign for 'dog'. It wasn't the same as in German sign language but it was so obvious that Tilly understood it.

'You know sign?' she signed to him, her heart racing. It would make such a difference if he could.

Michael signed that he knew a little. 'I learned at Scouts.'

Tilly nodded. Scouts had been banned in Germany years ago. The Hitler Youth had taken its place.

'Beautiful collar,' said Michael's mum, pointing at Wuffly's collar in the photograph so Tilly knew what she meant.

Tilly smiled and nodded. 'Beau-ti-ful collar,' she repeated hesitantly. 'Mutti . . .' and she pretended to sew.

Mrs Ward understood. 'Your mother made it for Wuffly?'

Tilly nodded.

'Mother at home in Germany?' Mrs Ward asked, and she put the fingertips of her two hands together with the palms open to make the shape of a roof. She'd learnt the sign for 'home' from Michael.

Tilly shook her head. An awful aching loneliness overcame her as she thought about her mum. Heggerty opened her eyes and rested her head on Tilly's knee as tears ran down Tilly's face.

Mrs Ward patted Tilly's hand. 'There, there,' she said.

Tilly mimed writing with a pen and then made the roof shape with her hands. 'I write home.' Michael wrote their address on one of the little pieces of paper he'd been using and gave it to her with a smile. Tilly made the sign for 'thank you' and then jumped up and hurried to her new room. They'd been given stamped notecards at Harwich so they could tell their families that they were safe and where they were staying in England. There was a pen on the bedside table.

The first card she wrote was to her father, Aunt Hedy and Oma.

My dearest family,

I am writing to you from London, an area called Wood Green, to let you know that I am now living with a family of animal lovers called the Wards. They have a son called Michael who is about the same age as me and who knows a little British Sign Language. It's not quite the same as German Sign Language, but it's not too different and so we are able to communicate a little that way. I now also know a handful of English words and am learning more all the time. Every time I use sign language I think of dear Opa and truly hope he is now back home with you. I hope more than anything that we are able to be together again some day soon.

Your loving daughter, Tilly

The door to her room was nudged open. Heggerty poked her nose in and the rest of her followed. She looked at Tilly and gave a slow tail wag as if asking permission to come in.

Tilly patted the bed next to her and Heggerty slowly climbed up.

'Good dog, Heggerty,' Tilly said as she brushed away the tears that ran down her face. If only Wuffly could be here too, lying on her bed like she used to.

Tilly picked up a second notecard and wrote to Gretchen and Wuffly.

Dear Gretchen

I hope Wuffly isn't being too much trouble. Sometimes in the morning my face is wet with tears and I remember that it is because I have been dreaming about her. Dear little Wuffly, the best dog in all the world. Be happy, Gretchen – that I do wish.

Your friend Tilly

PS I hope you had a lovely fourteenth birthday.

Tilly had only just finished writing her notecards when there was a rapping at the front door. She could hear someone speaking, but couldn't understand the words.

'I thought I'd pop in to say hello,' the woman at the front door told Mrs Ward. 'If you don't mind. I'm from the synagogue up the road and I speak a little German.'

'Of course we don't mind,' Mrs Ward said, opening the door widely.

'Tilly,' she called. 'Tilly, you have a visitor.' She ushered the visitor into the house. 'Now, how about some tea and cake?' she said.

Tilly came into the room as the lady sat down on the sofa.

'*Guten Tag*,' the lady said and Tilly's face burst into a smile. Michael and his dad were also there.

'You speak German?'

'Yes, my name's Olympia and I'm from the local synagogue. I'm checking in on all the *Kindertransport* children in this area, or as many of them as I can, to make sure they are settled. Although, this is only a short-term fostering. You'll be moving somewhere new soon.'

'Where will I go, then?' Tilly asked, worried.

But the lady didn't know. 'Maybe one of the Jewish hostels. Possibly the summer camp at Dovercourt.'

This was really bad news. She'd only just arrived and now she would have to move again.

'Do you have everything you need?' Olympia asked.

'Yes,' Tilly said. Then she remembered the cards she'd written. 'I have some notecards . . .'

'I'll post them for you, if you like,' Olympia said, and Tilly handed them over. 'Now how about English words you might need. Do you know the one for *toilet*, and how about *hungry* or *thirsty*, *tired*, *bed*, *cold*?'

Olympia gave Tilly a list of useful words in German with their English translation.

Mrs Ward brought in tea, cake and sandwiches. 'Help yourselves. There's plenty more if we need them.'

Olympia translated Tilly's story to the Wards so they would understand the circumstances that had brought her here and about her family.

'Wuffly sounds like a super sweet dog,' she said finally and Tilly nodded sadly.

'She is.'

'Now, is there anything you'd like to say to the Wards?' Olympia asked Tilly in German.

Tilly smiled and nodded. 'Thank you,' she said, although she already knew the English word for that. 'I would like to say thank you for making me feel so welcome.'

Olympia turned to Mrs Ward and asked if there was anything she'd like to say to Tilly. Mrs Ward nodded. 'We're very happy to have you here,' she said, and Olympia translated. 'And we hope you enjoy your stay with us. We wish it didn't have to be so brief.'

Michael nodded and so did his dad.

Olympia wrote her address on a piece of paper and gave it to Tilly. 'Any problems, you can ask for me at the synagogue or here's my home address. But I don't think you'll have any problems. They look like a wonderful family, I wish you could have stayed here for longer,' she said in German. 'But they're one of our short-term volunteer homes.'

Tilly nodded. Anyone who was lucky enough to stay with the Wards, even for a short time, was fortunate. But she was worried about where she would be sent next.

'Well, I'd better get on,' Olympia said. 'There's lots more children for me to check on and make sure that they're settled in.'

'Come again anytime,' Mrs Ward said as Olympia left.

Tilly burst into tears and hugged her.

'There now, now then,' Mrs Ward said. 'It's all right. There's no need for tears.'

Tilly tried to smile as she brushed them away. She didn't know enough English yet to tell Mrs Ward how much her generosity and kindness without prejudice meant. It had been so long since Tilly had felt accepted and safe.

Chapter 23

Soon Wuffly developed her own new daily routine.

Once Gretchen left for school, Wuffly ran off to spend the day with Hans, but she'd always be back waiting in the garden just before Gretchen came home. When Gretchen shut her in the playhouse for the night and went to bed, Wuffly would run to the cave and return before Gretchen awoke in the morning.

'That dog seems very well nourished for a stray that is not being fed much and is basically living in our yard,' Mrs Schmidt commented as she looked out at Wuffly from the kitchen window.

'I have to go to the German Girls' League,' Gretchen said, changing the subject. They'd been practising gymnastics for a big display in the new year.

'How's it going?' Fritz wanted to know. The Hitler Youth were taking part in the display too, but they weren't rehearsing together.

'It's OK,' Gretchen told him.

'Good. Make sure they put you at the front so everyone can see you. Tell them I'm your brother,' Fritz said.

Gretchen didn't like the ideals of the club. Especially when their gymnastics trainer kept going on about how bad Jewish people were. She was glad Tilly wasn't at her school now because she would have hated the horrid racist lessons they had almost everyday.

Gretchen usually sat by herself and when the others started singing their anti-Jewish songs or their Hitler fan club chants, she only pretended to join in.

She didn't like Nazi opinions, but her father had told her she had to keep going to the Hitler Girls' League regularly or they could all end up being sent to a disobedience camp. She did like the gymnastics, though – she always had, and she was good at it too.

'Don't expect me to keep watch over that mutt of yours while you're out,' Mrs Schmidt told her.

Gretchen sighed. 'I won't.' Her mother never did much more than look out of the window at Wuffly occasionally.

'I'll give the little dog some food later,' Fritz said.

Mrs Schmidt gave him an angry look.

'Scraps!' He laughed at her angry face. 'Just scraps. Better the dog has them than the rats.'

Mrs Schmidt looked like she wasn't sure about that.

Gretchen and Wuffly went out into the garden.

'Come on, Wuffly, in you go,' Gretchen said, and tempted the little dog into the vegetable shed (which her father had now fixed a lock on) with a bit of *bratwurst*. 'I'll be back soon.'

Wuffly did not like being shut in the shed, not one little bit. She tried barking to see if anyone would come and let her out, but no one did, not even the big angry lady. Then she tried whining, but that didn't work, either. The vegetable shed was a lot further away from the house than the playhouse had been and its single window was much higher. The shed did have more interesting smells, though, and a mouse family that lived under the withered tomato plants at the back of it.

Wuffly put her nose to the ground to get a better sniff, but none of the mice came out. Her paws dug at the earth to get closer to them. Outside, the ground was hard with the cold, but inside the shed the earth was soft because of the plants that had grown there.

The first tomato plant came up easily, and in no time at all, the second one was out too.

Wuffly's paws dug and dug as the soft earth went flying behind her into the shed. The hole she made wasn't huge, but it was big enough for a small and determined dog to squeeze through.

The German Girls' League gymnastics training session wasn't far from Grindel and, afterwards,

Gretchen decided to find out if there was any news about Tilly.

'What are you doing here?' Aunt Hedy asked when she opened the door. She looked around as she spoke as if worried someone might have followed Gretchen or be spying on her. 'You shouldn't be here. If the *Gestapo* sees . . .'

'They won't do anything,' Gretchen tried to reassure her.

But Aunt Hedy shook her head. 'Maybe they won't do anything to *you* in your German Girls' League uniform, but they'll do something to me. It's said thousands of Jews have been put into concentration camps . . . and more of them are being built all the time!'

'Neuengamme –' Gretchen began.

Hedy's eyes widened with fear. She put her finger to her lips as she nodded and beckoned Gretchen inside so she wouldn't be seen.

'Any Jewish person who can is getting out of Germany. But it's hard,' Hedy continued once they were inside and the door was closed. 'Mr Abrams is waiting in the long queues at different embassy gates to try and get visas for us. But other countries won't take us and legal immigration to Palestine is being limited.'

'I read in the paper that on *Kristallnacht*, thirty thousand Jewish men were arrested,' Gretchen said in a small voice.

Aunt Hedy nodded. 'And some of them were released only to be re-arrested,' she said. 'No one is safe who's Jewish or a friend of a Jew, or disabled in any way, or a traveller, or a communist, a Jehovah's Witness or anyone else Hitler doesn't like for any reason at all. They took a Catholic priest yesterday; they said he wasn't patriotic enough.'

Gretchen shuddered, remembering her father's tears. No one, it seemed, was truly safe.

'They say priests, both Protestant and Catholic, as well as nuns, are now being rounded up and put in camps,' Aunt Hedy said. 'I'm still hoping to get to Palestine one day, but it's looking so doubtful – and how can I possibly leave Oma behind?'

At the sound of her name there was a groan from one of the bedrooms. Gretchen followed Aunt Hedy to find Oma lying on the mattress on the floor. 'She barely speaks or moves now,' Aunt Hedy said. 'She no longer washes or gets dressed.'

'Mathilde?' Oma whispered, and Gretchen shook her head. She looked nothing like Tilly.

'Mr Abrams wrote Tilly a letter as soon as we learnt of her new address,' Hedy said. 'I'd like to give you a letter for her from me, too.'

'But I won't be seeing Tilly,' Gretchen said.

'No,' Hedy agreed, 'but a letter posted in your neighbourhood has more chance of being received by Tilly than one from Grindel. Will you take them?

I'll put both together in an envelope and attach a stamp for you.'

Gretchen nodded and Hedy went off to write her letter. Gretchen could hear her sniffing and blowing her nose every so often.

Aunt Hedy gave Gretchen a long, dark knitted scarf when she came back. 'Oma started knitting this for Tilly's fourteenth birthday, but after the pogrom . . .' Hedy sighed and shook her head. 'She did no more knitting after that. I finished it a few days ago. Here, you take it – it's starting to snow.

'Thank you,' Gretchen said. She took the scarf and put it round her head. Aunt Hedy gave her the envelope containing the letters from Tilly's father and herself.

'Take care of yourself, Gretchen,' Aunt Hedy said, as she saw her out.

'You too,' the girl replied, but the front door was already closed.

When Gretchen got home, her dad was sitting in the dark on a garden chair in the vegetable shed. Wuffly was next to him and his hand rested on the little dog's furry head.

'Dad, are you OK?' Gretchen asked.

'Just thinking,' her father said. 'Thinking about how a person, or even a few people, might escape from a train if it had a problem with the engine and had to stop in the woods, late at night.'

Gretchen frowned as he continued, 'A person might even find a small saw hidden and use it to remove the floorboards. They could use it to make a hole to the outside world and freedom.' He held up the small saw he'd used to make the shed more secure for Wuffly.

Her father looked at Gretchen and she looked back at him. Seconds passed.

'What if he were caught?' she said finally.

Her father stood up. 'Let's go and eat,' he said. 'Your mother's made a special supper to celebrate Fritz being selected for the Hitler school.'

First Tilly's gone and now Fritz, Gretchen thought as she shut a disappointed Wuffly in the shed. The little dachshund started whining and she could hear the sound of claws scratching. 'Be good, Wuffly,' Gretchen said as she followed her father inside. She wished Fritz didn't have to go away too.

Over dinner Gretchen told her parents how some of the older girls at the League of German Girls were going to apply for jobs in the camp.

'They said I should too, once I'm old enough.'

'You could do worse. It'll be regular, well-paid work,' Fritz said round a mouthful of schnitzel.

'No,' her father said to Gretchen. 'No, not you. I'd rather you left Germany forever than work there.'

'Of course she can't leave Germany,' Mrs Schmidt said. 'She'll get used to working at the camp. It's good money and respectable work. She should be grateful to have it and be supporting the *Führer*'s plans.' She gave her husband a pointed look.

But Gretchen's dad didn't pay any attention. He clasped Gretchen's hand.

Fritz frowned. 'Dad?'

'I mean it. People who work at the concentration camps gradually become like butchers or slaughterhouse workers. They stop seeing the person as a person. They stop seeing them even as a living being that should be treated with a fragment of kindness. Instead they are treated like walking waste.'

'That's not true,' said Fritz. 'Is it?' He looked over at his mother, who shrugged.

'What are you talking about, Dad?' Gretchen said. He was hurting her hand.

'Promise me you won't work at the new camp,' her father insisted. '*Promise me!*'

'I promise.'

Chapter 24

The next morning, Gretchen found the letter from Tilly torn in half and thrown in the bin.

'What's a letter addressed to me doing in here?' she demanded to know.

'You're better off now she's not having such a bad influence over you. Now the *Juden* girl's gone, you can be a proper German girl,' her mother told her as she sipped her coffee. She didn't look or sound the least bit guilty for having thrown Tilly's letter away. 'We have a good German son and now we'll have a good German daughter. Not a *Jude* befriender who could have ended up in a disobedience camp.'

Fritz came into the kitchen.

'There you are,' Mrs Schmidt smiled. 'What can I make you for breakfast before we set off for the school?'

'I'm not really hungry,' Fritz said, and Gretchen's eyes widened. Fritz was always hungry. He must be very nervous about going to his new school if he didn't want to eat.

'Oh, come now, you have to have something,' Mrs Schmidt said, standing up. 'I'll get out some cheeses and *liverwurst*. I bought some *schlackwurst* yesterday too . . .'

Fritz rolled his eyes and grinned at Gretchen and their dad as Mrs Schmidt brought out different breads and then set some eggs to boil.

After breakfast, it was time for Fritz and their mother to leave.

'Be good, little sister,' he told Gretchen as he wrapped his arms round her and squeezed.

'I'm always good.'

'Huh!'

He shook hands with his father, who then hugged him.

'Stay strong, son.'

'Yes, sir.'

'Time we were going,' said Mrs Schmidt as the taxi arrived.

Fritz wanted to say goodbye to Wuffly, but Mrs Schmidt said he'd get dog hair on his clothes, so he didn't.

When they'd gone, Gretchen took Tilly's letter outside to the vegetable shed, where Wuffly was, to read it in private.

A little while later her father came out into the garden to find her. 'How's Tilly doing over in England?' he asked.

'OK, I think,' Gretchen told him. She gave him Tilly's letter so he could read it too.

'Wood Green,' he said, noticing the address. 'I would have liked to visit London one day.'

'You will . . .' Gretchen said, but he just shook his head.

'Not now.'

'Tilly's mostly concerned about Wuffly,' Gretchen said, trying to lighten the mood.

The little dachshund looked up and wagged her tail at the sound of her name.

'I'm taking more children on the *Kindertransport* to the border with Holland later today,' her father said, handing the letter back.

Gretchen watched as he rubbed at the stubble on his chin. Not so long ago her father would have shaved the slightest bit of stubble before it had a chance to grow, but now he didn't care if he looked smart or not. Nowadays her dad often seemed lost, as if he'd seen too much and couldn't forget it.

'Sometimes I'm driving people to concentration camps, sometimes to a new life. Only a few weeks ago I was taking people to the last station in Germany before Poland, and watched as they were forced to walk through the snow, knowing they wouldn't be welcome once they got there. They have to pay, you know, to go on some of the trains I drive. Sometimes people come back, sometimes they don't. People need to travel and someone has to drive them. It might as well be me.'

'Dad . . .' Gretchen said. 'It's OK. It'll be all right.'

But her father just shook his head.

Gretchen was really worried about her dad. She and Wuffly followed him when he came out of the house wearing his railwayman's cap and coat a few hours later. He seemed so sad. She wanted her dad with the big belly laugh back.

'We'll come with you to the station,' she said, pulling on her coat and wrapping the black scarf that Aunt Hedy had given her around her head.

Her father didn't even seem to hear. He went to fetch his bike and Gretchen quickly scooped up Wuffly and put the little dog into the basket of her own bicycle.

'Wait for us, Dad!' she called out as her father set off. Gretchen pedalled quickly after him.

It was a cold, clear day and Gretchen was glad she was wearing the scarf that Oma had knitted. Wuffly held her head up in the basket as the wind sliced through her fur. They left the countryside and entered the bustle of central Hamburg and the train station.

When they arrived, Wuffly jumped out of the basket as Gretchen placed her bicycle next to her father's in the rack.

Mr Schmidt didn't wait for them. He didn't even seem to remember that they were with him. Gretchen didn't have time to take off her scarf as they followed him into the station.

This was the place Gretchen had last seen Tilly, when her friend had left on the *Kindertransport*. It was the last time Wuffly had seen her too. The little dog looked up at Gretchen and whined. 'It's OK, Wuffly,' Gretchen said.

Her father strode across the forecourt ahead of them. The station was full of children and their parents. People stretched out their hands to pet the dachshund, but Wuffly avoided them, her face intently looking all around for Tilly.

Gretchen heard children saying goodbye to their parents. Parents promising they'd be with their children again soon and trying not to let them see their tears.

She couldn't spot her father anywhere among the crowds. He must have made his way to the *Kindertransport* train already.

'Excuse me,' a lady said, bumping into Gretchen.

'It's all right,' Gretchen replied, but when she looked down she saw that Wuffly was gone.

'Wuffly, Wuffly!' she called out in a panic.

Then she caught sight of the dog in the distance, heading in the direction of the platforms. Gretchen tried to push through the crowd to reach her. 'Excuse me, excuse me.'

Ahead of her she could see Wuffly's little body amid the sea of moving shoes. But people didn't want to get out of the way or let Gretchen past. Every moment with their children was too precious.

'*Parents, leave your children and stay behind the wooden barrier,*' the voice over the tannoy said. '*Children, make your way to the platform.*'

Wuffly ran through the crush and along the platform. The smell of coal being burnt to fuel the steam train's engine filled her sensitive nostrils.

A large lady was organizing the children and helping to get them on board the train.

'Don't worry,' she said to the parents. 'I'm Truus Wijsmuller from Holland. I will see that your children arrive safely. I know it's hard, but you are doing the best thing for your little ones. Come on, children – this way now.'

She herded the scared, bewildered and sometimes excited youngsters towards the train.

On the platform, a train door opened and, quick as a flash, Wuffly was up the steps and onboard.

'A dog!' one of the smaller children said eagerly. 'A dog's coming with us.'

But the train was so noisy and everyone was talking at once so nobody paid much attention.

'Wuffly, come back! Wuffly!' Gretchen's mouth fell open as she saw the little dog jump up the steps and on to the train. 'Wuffly, *no*!'

Gretchen ran on to the train after her. 'Have you seen a small dog?' she asked the children waving goodbye to their parents in the first carriage. None of them had.

'Anyone seen a dog?' she asked the same question of a teenage girl holding a baby wrapped in a shawl, in the carriage opposite.

'Dogs aren't allowed on the train,' the girl said, looking worried. 'We all have to obey the rules.'

Gretchen moved on, but then she heard the distinctive whistle. The train was getting ready to leave.

'Why are you not in your seat?' barked a huge German soldier with a big moustache and a gun at his hip.

'You are not allowed to walk about in the corridors,' said a second soldier behind him, also carrying a gun.

Gretchen didn't want to be shot.

'I'm looking . . .' Gretchen started to explain, but the soldiers didn't care what she had to say. One of them opened the nearest compartment door and pushed her roughly inside . . . so hard that she fell on the ground.

'Be quiet, *Jude*!'

Gretchen was going to protest that she wasn't Jewish, but she was too frightened to say anything and they probably wouldn't believe her anyway.

'My father –'

One of the soldiers struck her across the face so hard that she bit her tongue and her mouth started to bleed.

'No more talking!' they said as they left.

Gretchen wiped at her mouth and then jumped up and opened the compartment door. Two different soldiers were chatting at the end of the corridor. Fortunately they were facing the other way.

Gretchen tried to open the outside door to the platform but couldn't. She tried again. It must be locked from the outside. But why would it be locked?

Gretchen bit her bottom lip, then pushed the window down so she could try and open the door from the other side, but it still wouldn't budge.

Outside there was a lady holding a baby.

'Take my baby. Please take my baby,' the woman said, pushing the baby through the window into a bewildered Gretchen's arms.

'I can't . . .' Gretchen said in alarm, not quite knowing how to hold the baby properly.

'She'll be killed if you don't,' the woman said, disappearing into the throng of people before Gretchen knew what was happening.

Gretchen looked down at the child, who gurgled up at her. 'What on earth am I going to do with you?' she said.

'Back inside!' yelled one of the soldiers who'd had his back turned earlier. He waved his hand at the door Gretchen had just come out of. '*Now!*'

Gretchen went back into the compartment with the baby and sat down.

The soldier followed her inside. 'Don't leave again or I'll shoot,' he warned.

Gretchen nodded and pulled the dark scarf more tightly round her hair with her free hand.

The soldier didn't say anything about the baby she was holding.

Gretchen could barely breathe, didn't breathe, in fact, until he pulled the door closed. Her heart felt like it was thumping in her throat instead of her chest. The baby looked up at her and smiled.

The other children in the compartment all stared at Gretchen.

'Brave,' one of them said.

'Foolish,' commented another.

Chapter 25

Gretchen was still looking down at the baby in her lap as the train's whistle blew and it left the station. The infant's tiny hands reached out to grab the scarf hiding her blonde hair. Gretchen's face hurt from where the soldier had struck her.

The Nazis shouldn't be allowed to do things like that, she told herself. But even as she was thinking it, she realized the Nazis could do whatever they liked. No one could protest or make a fuss without ending up in a worse situation. At least she knew her father was driving the train. He'd be able to sort everything out – if she could only get to him.

The compartment door slid open.

'Chaperone?' an SS soldier said, nodding at the baby she was holding, then back at Gretchen.

Gretchen didn't know what to say. She wasn't a chaperone. She didn't have any papers and she shouldn't even be on the train.

'Are you a chaperone – you *dummkopf Jude*?' the soldier shouted.

The baby started wailing as Gretchen nodded. What else could she do? The baby cried louder and louder.

'Shut it up or I'll throw it out of the window,' the soldier threatened, and with that he stomped from the compartment just as Truus Wijsmuller came rushing in.

'Why isn't this child with the other babies?' she asked.

Gretchen looked worried. 'Her mother handed her to me through the window just now. She doesn't have any papers. I don't . . .'

Truus looked behind her to make sure there were no more soldiers in the corridor, then she nodded and took the baby from Gretchen. 'I'll take her to the right compartment. Thank you for looking after her.'

Gretchen sat down again, but kept glancing at the door, expecting at any moment that more soldiers would come and arrest her.

Her mother's warnings about the special prison camps for wayward German girls rang in her ears. She was pretty sure that being on a train meant for Jewish children with a runaway dog and a baby that shouldn't have been there would count as wayward.

Fritz and her mother must be at the Hitler boarding school by now. They'd be horrified if they knew where she was.

The other children in the compartment were still gazing at her. Then one of them opened his suitcase and pulled out a bag of sandwiches. Then the others opened theirs to see what had been packed for them and brought out little cakes and more sandwiches.

The first boy offered his food bag to Gretchen.

'No, it's OK,' she said, not wanting to take anything. He might be hungry later.

'Go on,' he urged her. 'They're good.'

Gretchen took the smallest sandwich. 'Thanks.'

Three compartments along from Gretchen, Wuffly was hidden under the train seats. No one knew she was there, but when the children opened their luggage and started tucking into tasty chicken sandwiches, boiled eggs and cakes, the smell was too much for her to resist.

She crept out, much to the delight of the young passengers.

'Here, little dog,' they said as they stroked her and offered small bits of their food.

Wuffly wagged her tail.

'She's so sweet,' they said delightedly.

When the Nazi officers came into their compartment, the children had no food left and Wuffly was back in her hiding place under the seats.

The bullying soldiers had quickly become impatient with terrified children crying and screaming and taking ages to open their suitcases. So now they just did it themselves, dumping everything on the floor, stamping on it and marching out again.

Wuffly crept out from her hiding place once they'd gone and the children stroked her as they put their few belongings back into their suitcases.

Every glass frame of every photo had been smashed, but at least the pictures of loved ones within them remained. 'They didn't have to break everything,' a little boy said miserably.

Stuck in her compartment and not daring to leave, Gretchen thought about where Wuffly could be. What would the soldiers do if they found her? Would they keep her? She was a beautiful dog, usually well behaved and in very good condition. She assumed they'd probably keep her as their own dog. Or at least protect her. Animal protection was taught in all public schools and universities now.

Hours later the train stopped at the border and the Nazi soldiers got off.

Gretchen could see them through the window, laughing and joking with each other.

She saw her father walking down the platform towards the train he would now be driving back to Hamburg. Gretchen banged on the window to attract his attention, but he didn't look over at her and carried on his way.

The Nazi soldiers saw her, though, and came over to the window. They poked out their tongues and one of them lifted his gun and pointed it at her as the other soldiers laughed.

The train crossed the border to Holland with Gretchen still on board.

Once they reached Oldenzaal, the first station in Holland, the train stopped again. Kind ladies brought the children drinks and food. But Gretchen was still worried. What was going to happen when they discovered she shouldn't have been on board? That she didn't have any papers or money or even a change of clothes?

Now they were in Holland, the children were allowed to move about the train. Gretchen went up and down the corridor looking for Wuffly, but she couldn't see her anywhere. The soldiers must have taken her. Maybe she was already on her way back to Germany. Gretchen felt utterly disheartened.

Back in the compartment, Gretchen closed her eyes and thought of her father. Would he really try to help the people he was supposed to be taking to the concentration camps escape? He'd looked so determined that she thought he just might.

She could picture her father loosening the floorboards of the trains people were crammed into. She could imagine him stopping the train late at night because of some supposed problem with the engine or the railway tracks.

Maybe most of the Nazi soldiers would be asleep in the comfortable carriages reserved for them when the train stopped. They would probably have been served food and wine. They'd be resting their heads comfortably on their cushioned seats. Unlike the people imprisoned in the third-class compartments or even cattle trucks with no seats to sit on and no room to lie down. Not even any water to drink.

She hoped one of them managed to prise up a floorboard. Then discover that the floorboards next to it were also loose. That some of the prisoners managed to drop through the hole on to the tracks while the train was stationary, before disappearing into the woods beyond.

When they arrived at the Hook of Holland, Wuffly slipped unseen up the gangplank and on to the giant ship amid the many legs and suitcases of the children.

Already on board, Gretchen stared through the gaps at the water churning below her. She'd never been on a ship before and it made her tummy feel funny.

They were given tasteless white bread to eat instead of the delicious black bread she was used to at home, and something called marmalade that was sharp on her tongue and she wasn't sure she liked. But the worst thing, the very worst thing, was a brown water that you poured milk into and was called 'tea'. None of the other children seemed to like it either, and around her they pulled faces as they took a mouthful and forced themselves to swallow it.

The ferry swayed back and forth in the waves and Gretchen went outside on to the deck because she was feeling sick. And it was there, under a wooden bench, that Gretchen at last found her lost dachshund, shaking with fear from the unfamiliar violence of the waves that crashed around her.

'Oh, Wuffly,' Gretchen said gently as she knelt down beside her. She held the little dog close and hid her inside her coat as the ferry reached England.

Chapter 26

Hans liked the little dog's visits and when Wuffly didn't come, he missed her. As he ate his breakfast of fish, he wondered where she was and what she was doing. He saved her a bit for later and then headed through the forest to the house where she lived. When he got there he stayed hidden in the trees and watched and waited.

The windows upstairs that the woman usually opened were all closed today. There was a stillness and emptiness about the place. Hans's instincts told him it was empty, but still he kept watch for a long while to be sure.

At last he was confident enough to run over to the playhouse where the little dog was sometimes kept. Checking behind him first, he pulled open the door, but there was no sign that she had been there recently. Then he headed over to the vegetable shed but she wasn't there, either.

Finally he went back to the main house and crept all around it until he found a way in through a window that had been left open a crack.

It was warm inside the house compared to outside. The remnants of a fire smouldered in the hearth. In the kitchen he found a loaf of bread. He cut a chunk off and ate it slathered with jam.

Upstairs he saw the soft warm beds where the family had slept. He pulled a face at the pictures, many from newspapers, of Hitler's smug face on the boy's bedroom walls. There was also an engraved trophy for being the best fighter at the Hitler Youth camp – *Fritz Schmidt 1938.*

Next to the trophy was a diary. Hans read snippets of it as he turned the pages, learning what life was like for a privileged boy in the Hitler Youth. A boy who wouldn't be killed or experimented on just because he was deaf.

Hans put the diary back, then opened the door of the wardrobe and stared at the clothes inside. Then he went into the other rooms of the house and even up into the attic, but the little dog wasn't anywhere to be found.

Maybe the family had gone away on a trip for the day and taken her with them.

Hans helped himself to a large rucksack and stuffed it full of food and blankets, hats, scarves and socks. Lots of socks. His feet were always getting soaked. Fritz's thick, warm, home-made woollen socks would keep the cold out. Hans grinned with delight when he saw that Fritz and he were roughly the same shoe size. Now he had a new pair of winter boots to wear as well.

Hans made his way back to the cave in the woods with his treasures.

It was late at night and there was a full moon when the train stopped on the tracks close to the woods. Some of the prisoners had started pulling up the floorboards as soon as someone realized they were loose. Then someone else had found the small saw. The already cramped, beaten, hungry, thirsty and exhausted occupants pressed themselves against the sides of the carriage away from the activity that was taking place. No one knew where they were or even how briefly the train would stop here. So they had to work fast, they had to be ready. They stared at the widening hole in the floorboards and then at each other. This was hope.

Before they'd been shut in, some had been led to believe they were going to a better place – a work camp, where the manual labour would be hard, but they would be treated well.

Once they got on to the train, however, those final hopes had been crushed.

They'd been crammed inside a train carriage and forced to stand because there were no seats; there was no water, either. Just barbed wire at the windows, a single bucket between them for toilet facilities and no way to get out.

There'd been rumours that what they were being told were lies, but people hadn't wanted to believe it. They'd wanted to believe there was finally something good about to happen after the years of hardship.

Now they stared at the hole in the floorboards, mesmerized. Hope had returned.

When the train had been racing along the tracks it would have been too dangerous, almost certain death, to try and escape.

But now the train had stopped they had to take their chance.

First one man went down through the hole they'd made, then more people quickly followed and ran towards the cover of the trees.

The cattle trucks, where the prisoners were kept, were located right at the back of the train; the guards, meanwhile, were asleep or dozing off in their luxury passenger compartment further up.

At first the soldiers weren't concerned by the stop, but after a while they started getting suspicious.

'Hey!'

'*Was ist das?*'

'Why have we stopped?'

One of them pulled on his thick winter coat and headed to the driver's cabin at the front of the train.

The train driver apologized. He thought he'd seen something blocking the line ahead, but it was dark, especially when the clouds covered the full moon. He'd thought it was a cow or a horse, but he could have been mistaken. Or maybe it had been there, but was now gone.

The soldier commanded him to drive on immediately. There was no time to waste. So the train started up again and gradually gained speed as it headed onwards.

Hans saw the bewildered, frightened escapees as they came into the safety of the woods. They were so thirsty they gulped water direct from the stream in the moonlight, close to his mud Golem. They huddled together for warmth until they finally fell asleep. Even the snow that came fluttering down through the trees couldn't keep them awake.

Hans stayed hidden and didn't approach them. It was hard to make himself understood by hearing people who had no knowledge of sign language. He didn't need their company. He was fine on his own.

But when he saw a lady sob uncontrollably, shivering with the cold, he stood up straight. There *was* something he could do to help them.

He ran silently back through the trees to Gretchen's house, which was in darkness, and pushed up the window.

When the escaped prisoners woke up the next morning they found a small fire burning close by.

Warm coats and jumpers and shoes lay next to it. And food – the best of German foods – was piled high.

'How can this be?'

'It's like a miracle,' they whispered to each other.

They looked at the roughly shaped Golem in the stream. Who could have done this for them?

Chapter 27

It wasn't until the *Kindertransport* children got off the ferry at snowy Harwich that Gretchen was properly stopped and questioned.

'Where's your white card?' the official asked her in English, pointing to the other children around her and holding up an example of what he wanted. Passports and visas had been suspended, but white cards had been given out instead and the officials were checking them and making a note of the children's names in a book.

Other children had identity cards, labels round their necks, but Gretchen didn't. Her heart raced. What would happen when they found she didn't have one? Would she be sent back to Germany and a camp for disobedience, or would she be put in prison over here?

'White card?' the official repeated very slowly.

Gretchen shook her head because she didn't have one.

But at that moment Wuffly poked her head through the buttons of Gretchen's coat to see what was going on.

The official's eyes almost popped out of his head when he saw her.

'*A dog!* You have a dog! You are not allowed to bring a dog!' he shouted, his face going almost as red as the angry German soldiers' faces had done on the train.

Gretchen couldn't see the official's gun, but that didn't mean he didn't have one.

'Rabies, rabies!' he yelled.

Gretchen couldn't understand what he was saying and she was very frightened.

Wuffly was terrified by all the shouting too. She could feel Gretchen's heart racing and she could smell her fear. Gretchen's terror infected the little dog and she jumped out of her coat and ran.

'Stop!' the official yelled. 'Stop that dog!'

'Wuffly,' Gretchen called after her as the little dog went running under chairs and between surprised people. 'Wuffly, come back!'

She tried to go after her, but the official grabbed her arm.

'No!'

A translator called Mrs Harris hurried over to Gretchen. The angry official let go of her arm and moved away.

'Is that your dog?' Mrs Harris asked Gretchen in German as she pointed in the direction that Wuffly had gone.

Gretchen shook her head. Wuffly was Tilly's dog.

'It will be put down if it doesn't belong to anyone,' Mrs Harris said. 'It won't be quarantined if it's just a stray. We can't take the risk of rabies.' The word for rabies in German was *tollwut*.

'Wuffly doesn't have rabies!' Gretchen gasped, horrified at the idea. No wonder everyone had been in such a panic if they thought that.

'We can't be sure,' Mrs Harris told her.

But Gretchen *was* sure. 'Wuffly hasn't been anywhere other than on a train with children and then a boat. She can't have rabies.'

'How do you know? You said she didn't belong to you.'

'Wuffly belongs to my friend Tilly. She came over on the *Kindertransport* a few weeks ago. She's already in England,' Gretchen told her.

Mrs Harris sighed. There were so many *Kindertransport* children to try and process and it had been a very long day.

Gretchen had Tilly's letter in her pocket and not much else. She handed it to Mrs Harris and pointed at her friend's new address. 'Tilly's staying here. She'll tell you that Wuffly's her dog and that she doesn't have rabies.'

'And is Wuffly registered in Germany?' Mrs Harris asked.

'Yes,' Gretchen said, although she didn't know absolutely. She was sure Tilly's family would have paid for the *Hundesteuer*, or dog licence.

Mrs Harris still looked doubtful.

'Is this where you will be staying too?' she asked Gretchen.

Gretchen looked over at the angry official who'd asked for her white card that she didn't have. He was talking to another man in a uniform.

Gretchen nodded.

'I'll need to find someone to take you there,' Mrs Harris said, looking around. 'We need urgent confirmation that the dog is registered and belongs to your friend. Otherwise . . .'

'What about Wuffly?' Gretchen asked.

Mrs Harris shook her head. 'We take the risk of rabies from foreign dogs very seriously. The dog will be taken to the quarantine kennels in Epping until we get to the bottom of this.'

'But she'll be so frightened.'

They wouldn't really put Wuffly down, would they? Not Wuffly. She was so small and sweet. She had done nothing wrong other than try to find the person she loved.

Mrs Harris shook her head. 'Better frightened than dead,' she said.

A man headed over to them. 'Let's get this mess sorted out,' he said. Mrs Harris translated so Gretchen would know what was happening and showed him Tilly's address on Gretchen's letter. 'I know the area.'

The man didn't speak German so they didn't talk on the journey to London, but he drove fast through the snowy streets and for that Gretchen was grateful. She needed to get to Tilly as soon as possible. They had to save Wuffly!

*

More people started to chase after Wuffly, which only made everything worse. She ran and ran but they cornered the dachshund and she dived under some chairs placed against a wall in an empty waiting room. The people chasing her pushed the chairs out of the way, scraping them noisily against the floor as they came closer.

Big hands. Big feet. Fingers reaching towards her.

'Be careful, it could bite,' a voice said.

Wuffly cowered further under the chairs, trying to make her little body as small as she could. Her whole body was shaking now and she whined and whimpered with fear.

Hands wearing bite-proof gloves stretched towards the terrified little dog. A stick with a hook on the end of it caught on her collar and pulled her forward.

She was pushed into a small cage that was lifted up and put into the back of an RSPCA van.

'What a pretty little dog,' the port vet said when she came to check on Wuffly before she was taken to the kennels. 'She belongs to one of the *Kindertransport* children, I'm told.'

'No one knows for absolute sure. The girl who smuggled her in said the dog's name was Wuffly but it hasn't been officially claimed yet,' an RSPCA worker told her.

If dogs weren't claimed, the quarantine kennels couldn't look after them. They were too full as it was.

'She doesn't look like a stray,' the vet said as she pulled on her protective gloves. 'She looks like someone's much-loved pet.'

The vet shone a light from a little torch into Wuffly's brown eyes, and checked her over to see if she was sore anywhere. She looked in her mouth, took her temperature and finally listened to her heart and lungs with a stethoscope.

'She seems perfectly healthy,' the vet said at the end of the examination. 'I can almost guarantee she doesn't have rabies, but she'll have to remain in quarantine, of course.' That was the law.

Then the vet went off to inspect two racehorses that had been brought over on a ship.

Wuffly blinked when the doors of the van were closed and everything went dark. She wasn't used to motor vehicles. Usually she travelled in a bicycle basket, if she wasn't walking or running instead. But in the last few days, she'd been on a train, a boat and now she was in a van!

She didn't like the strong smell of petrol as the van started up and she didn't like the way it rolled and rattled as it drove along. Most of all she didn't like being caught. She wanted to be back with Tilly in Grindel, or in the woods with Hans, or even eating sausages at the grumpy lady's house with Gretchen.

When the van finally pulled up at the quarantine kennels hours later, Wuffly didn't even sit up.

'Is this dog sick?' one of the kennel maids asked.

Wuffly blinked at the sudden burst of light from the now open van.

'She seems very lethargic,' said another of the kennel maids, called Clara. 'Does anyone know her name?'

'Wuffly,' the driver of the van told her, getting out and blowing on his hands. It was freezing outside.

From inside her cage, Wuffly's dark, intelligent eyes could see the woodlands covered in snow beyond the kennel gates. Woodlands that were not dissimilar to the ones where Hans lived.

'I'm opening the cage to take a closer look,' Clara said. 'Hello, Wuffly.'

'Make sure you wear protective gloves,' the van driver warned her. 'The vet checked her over at the port and said she seemed perfectly healthy, but you can never be completely sure. A little dog could be infected with rabies just as easily as a big dog.'

As the cage door was opened Wuffly jumped up and raced past Clara's gloved hands as they came towards her. All Clara managed to get hold of was Wuffly's red-and-gold collar, which came off in her hand.

'Quick, stop her!' Clara shouted.

There was a fraction of a second of hesitation because no one wanted to get too close to a dog that might have rabies. That brief window of time was enough for Wuffly to run out of the gates, over the road and into the trees beyond. They were too late.

The kennel staff pulled on their gloves. One picked up a net.

'We have to find her,' Clara said, still holding Wuffly's collar. 'She could be infectious.'

'Could infect livestock,' another of the kennel staff said as they made for the woods after Wuffly.

'We can't take the risk,' Clara said.

'There's no cure for rabies.'

'She'll have to be shot if we can't get close enough,' one of the other kennel staff said gravely, and she went back to get the gun.

Chapter 28

At number 39, Tilly packed the last of her few belongings into her small suitcase. It was time to leave the Wards and move on to her next home, although she didn't know how long she'd be there either. Maybe this was what it was going to be like from now on. Arriving and moving on until one day, maybe, she could go back to Germany or her family could come to England.

She clutched the two letters she'd had from home so far. It was such a relief to know her father, Aunt Hedy and Oma were all OK. She'd read the letter from her father so many times she could almost recite it by heart.

My dearest Mathilde,

I cannot tell you how much we miss you here, but also how pleased we are to think you are now safe in England. I hope to send you many more letters, until the time that we meet again.

Your loving father

Aunt Hedy had sent greetings from Oma as well as herself. She was still hoping to go to Palestine one day and urged Tilly to be brave and well behaved in her new country. *'Make us proud xx'*

Once Tilly knew where she was staying next, she'd send them more letters with her new address. Mrs Ward and Olympia had said they would forward any that arrived here after she'd left as well. She didn't want to miss even one.

Tilly wished there'd been a letter from Gretchen too, but there'd been nothing from her so far. And no news of Wuffly. Maybe she and Gretchen really weren't friends any more. Maybe they never would be again.

She felt sad as she thought back to her school in Hamburg and how much better it had been because Gretchen was there too, when they were still best friends. It felt like a very long time ago now.

Tilly had been really worried about what would happen when she went to school in England, but luckily she'd had Michael with her. Plus there were two younger children, Udo and Freda, who'd come over on the *Kindertransport*. They were temporarily staying with the rabbi at the synagogue.

Olympia had come into the school every morning to help them practise their English, but during breaks and at lunchtime all the children at the school played together in the playground. It was very different from what Udo and Freda had been used to.

'At my old school the other children threw stones at me,' Udo said.

'I wasn't allowed to play in the playground,' Freda said as another girl beckoned her over to join in with a game of skipping.

Tilly still missed having Gretchen in the class with her. They'd always spend breaktimes together. She wondered what her next school would be like. Maybe there wouldn't even be one. In Germany, children went to school until they were eighteen, but in England it was different. Compulsory education was only up to the age of fourteen. Olympia said that some of the children her age who'd come over to England were already at work.

'All right, dear?' Mrs Ward said, coming into Tilly's room.

Tilly nodded and brushed away a tear.

'I'll miss you,' she said.

Mrs Ward had been unfailingly kind. She'd even made her a surprise tea on her birthday a few days ago.

'And I'll miss you,' Mrs Ward said, 'but we can still keep in touch. I've brought you one of Michael's sweaters in case you're cold in your next house. Some places can be dreadfully cold. And I made you this,' she said, giving Tilly a long colourful knitted scarf. 'I'm sorry I couldn't get it finished in time for your birthday. But it's done now.'

'Thank you,' Tilly smiled as she wrapped it round her neck.

Just at that moment, a rhythmic knocking at the front door, consisting of two slow raps followed by three quicker ones, made them both jump.

'That must be the transport to your new lodgings,' Mrs Ward said, picking up Tilly's suitcase for her.

But Tilly knew it wasn't. She raced down the stairs, opened the door and stared at the tall, bedraggled blonde girl and the man standing next to her.

'*Gretchen!*' Tilly gasped in surprise, throwing her arms round her friend.

Mrs Ward followed her down the stairs. 'May I help you?' she said to the man.

'It's about a dog,' the man told her.

Mrs Ward looked confused. 'So you're not the transport for Tilly?'

'Wuffly's in danger!' Gretchen said to Tilly. 'You have to come.'

Mrs Ward looked from one girl to the other as they spoke in very fast German. She hardly understood a word, apart from *Herr Hitler*, of course. Everyone knew that name.

Fortunately, the man explained what had happened, as far as he knew, in English.

'She must have brought the little dog over from Germany hidden in her coat. You'll need to go to the quarantine kennels in Epping as quick as you can to identify it, if you want to keep it. That's where it will have been taken once it's caught. Anyway, I've got to be getting back to Harwich. There's more *Kindertransport* children due in later and who knows what they'll be trying to bring in with them!'

Michael and Mr Ward came to join Tilly, Gretchen and Mrs Ward as the man drove off.

'What's going on?' Michael asked.

'We have to go to the quarantine kennels at Epping!' Mrs Ward told him. 'Tilly's dog, Wuffly, could be put down if we don't.'

'All dogs coming in from overseas have to be quarantined,' Mr Ward explained. He looked worried. 'Was Wuffly wearing a collar?'

He mimed collar to Gretchen and she nodded.

'Thank goodness,' he said. Dogs without collars were in far greater danger of being put down.

Tilly took her coat off the rack. It had her little Golem in one pocket and Wuffly's original name tag that the Hitler Youth boy had thrown on the ground and broken in the other.

'Please,' said Tilly. 'Please may we go to the quarantine kennels now?' She had to see poor Wuffly. The little dog must be so confused. She opened her hand to show them the name tag. 'And there's proof on her collar, if she still has it, that she's mine and registered.'

'Of course,' said Mr Ward.

'We must,' said Mrs Ward.

'Have to,' agreed Michael.

Mrs Ward left a note on the front door for Tilly's transport to say they had an emergency to deal with and they'd be back later, then they all climbed into the RSPCA truck and set off to rescue Wuffly.

Tilly had so much to tell Gretchen and her friend had just as much to say.

Tilly's hair had already grown back a little bit since Gretchen had last seen her. She could now tie it in a tiny ponytail.

'I like your scarf,' Tilly said.

'Aunt Hedy gave it to me,' Gretchen told her. 'Oma made it for you, really. I like yours too.'

'Mrs Ward made it for me,' Tilly told her. She was going to miss staying with the Wards and all their animals.

They headed out of North London, where people's feet turned the snow into grey slush, towards the white-covered countryside of Essex.

'At least my father, Aunt Hedy and Oma are OK,' Tilly said. 'They wrote to let me know.' She wiped her eyes with the end of her new scarf. She missed them so much.

When Tilly's tears had stopped, she stared out of the window at the fields they drove past. Gretchen didn't say anything.

'I'm sorry I was so mean the last time we met. I'd just been hurt by some Hitler Youth boys,'

Tilly told Gretchen a while later. 'They cut off my hair.'

'I know!' Gretchen said. 'I threw my shoe at them and then cycled away as fast as I could. I was bringing Wuffly back to you. She was in my room when I woke up that morning. Fritz knew the boy who'd taken her. But I knew I couldn't keep her.'

Tilly was shaking her head. 'I didn't realize,' she said. 'I couldn't think how she'd managed to come back to me. As I was running from the boys, I looked over my shoulder and there she was running after me! When I brought Wuffly to your house on the day I was leaving on the *Kindertransport*, I gave her to Fritz. He made me promise I'd never go back to your house or try to contact you. I knew that being with you would be the safest thing for Wuffly, so I agreed. I didn't have a choice. Although I really wanted to see you – I missed not seeing you so much.'

'And I missed you!' said Gretchen. 'I missed you every single day.'

Chapter 29

Hidden among the leafless trees and brown fronded ferns, Wuffly watched as the kennel staff searched for her. Her black-and-tan coat was the perfect camouflage in the winter forest.

'Wuffly!'

'Wu-ff-ly, where are you?' voices called to her.

But the voices weren't familiar and the little dog didn't go to them.

At last they stopped calling her, but she waited and listened to be sure they'd really gone. Only then did she come out and start exploring her new surroundings.

The pond in the centre of the forest was much larger and had lots more fish in it than Hans's stream. Parts of it were frozen over, but not all of the water was covered in ice. In no time at all, Wuffly had swum out and caught herself a small trout.

Hans had always cooked the fish they caught, but Wuffly found she liked the taste of raw fish just as much.

When she'd finished eating, she found a comfortable spot in a fallen hollow tree, curled up and went to sleep.

As the disappointed kennel staff headed back through the woods without Wuffly, Clara looked at the little dog's red-and-gold collar. It was such a shame they hadn't been able to catch her. She must be so frightened, lost and alone in the forest.

Clara didn't think the dachshund had rabies – it was very rare, although very dangerous too. The last infection in the UK had been back in 1922, and they certainly didn't want another one.

As she walked she opened Wuffly's locket and smiled when she saw the little dog's name written on the heart-shaped card. There was something behind it, though, wedged between the number disc – another piece of paper, folded up very small.

Clara frowned as she unfolded it and then gasped. Her supervisor, Mrs Bronson, *needed* to see this.

Back at work, Clara found Mrs Bronson putting a tin bowl of water in a Great Dane's kennel. The dog immediately started drinking thirstily, some of the water running out of his giant slobbery mouth as he did so.

'Wuffly means *woof* in German,' Clara told Mrs Bronson.

Clara had come over from Austria on a domestic permit when the kennels had put an advert in the newspaper for more staff. Austria and Nazi Germany had become annexed in March and many Jewish girls and women had got out as soon as they could, including Clara. But you had to have a domestic work permit.

'Does it indeed?' said Mrs Bronson, brushing down her suit.

'Wuffly came over with the *Kindertransport*,' Clara said.

Mrs Bronson nodded. 'Quarantine for six months, then.'

'Yes, only she's escaped and is lost in the forest.'

Mrs Bronson looked very worried. 'Then we need to find her as soon as possible.'

A missing dog was the last thing they needed. Flu had been going round the staff and everyone was having to take on extra duties. Plus there'd been a big influx of dogs needing shelter since the threat of war at the end of September. People were panicking that there was going to be another war and moving out of London if they could. The kennels were fit to bursting already!

Clara handed the supervisor Wuffly's red-and-gold collar.

'Beautiful craftwork. Looks home-made,' Mrs Bronson said.

Clara nodded and took a deep breath. 'And I found *this* inside the locket attached to the little dog's collar.' She handed the supervisor the folded paper with Hans's drawing on it.

'It looks like some sort of map,' Mrs Bronson said.

Clara nodded again. 'It appears to be a map of an army base or camp,' she said.

'Do you know where Neuengamme is?' Mrs Bronson asked. She pointed at the word Hans had written.

'*Neuengamme* – it's on the outskirts of Hamburg,' Clara said. 'I wonder what the map was doing hidden in the dog's locket?'

'I think we'd better pass this on to the authorities,' said the supervisor. 'You keep looking for the missing dog.'

Clara went back to the forest.

Two men from Army Intelligence turned up in less than an hour to look at the hand-drawn map. Clara, who was still in the forest searching unsuccessfully for the missing dog with some of the other kennel staff, was called back and taken to Mrs Bronson's office.

'You found this hidden in a dog's collar, you say?' the Intelligence officers asked her.

Clara nodded. 'It was inside a locket hidden behind a card with the dog's name – Wuffly – written on it.'

The two men pored over the map with their magnifying glasses. They seemed very excited about the information Wuffly had inadvertently brought to England with her.

'Intelligence like this about hidden camps is just what we need,' one of the officers explained.

'Are you monitoring the Nazis, then?' Clara asked.

Hitler had done so many dreadful things since he'd come to power that Clara thought nobody even noticed any more.

'Of course we are.'

'Surreptitiously, of course.'

'Do you know anything else about where the little dog that brought this came from?'

No one yet knew exactly whose dog Wuffly was.

'The girl who was with her at Harwich said the animal wasn't hers, but she wasn't a stray, either,' Clara told the men.

'Just as well the dog wasn't discovered until they left the ferry. If they'd still been in Germany, or even Holland, it would have been detained and we wouldn't have this invaluable information.'

When Tilly, Gretchen and the Wards arrived at the kennels an hour after they'd left Wood Green, they were immediately taken to see the men from Army Intelligence in the supervisor's office.

'How did a map of a Nazi camp end up inside your dog's locket?' the officers asked Tilly and

Gretchen. They spoke a little German, but not as much as Clara, who was fluent in both languages and translated for them.

'I don't know,' Tilly said. She couldn't sit still. 'Can I see Wuffly now?'

'Once you've answered our questions.'

'I don't know, either. I've never opened Wuffly's locket,' Gretchen told the men as Clara translated what she said.

Tilly bit her bottom lip. She hadn't seen Wuffly for so long and now these men were holding up their reunion. It wasn't fair.

'My mother gave me the locket before she died,' Tilly said. 'I put Wuffly's name inside it after she was taken from me. I found her number identity disc on the ground on *Kristallnacht*. Her name tag was broken.'

'But you've never seen this map before?'

'No,' Tilly said.

'And you've no idea who hid it in the locket?'

Tilly shook her head again and then frowned. There was something familiar about it. 'May I take a closer look?' she asked, suddenly interested.

'It's a detailed drawing of a camp close to Neuengamme,' one of the men said as he handed it to her.

'Oh,' Tilly said. 'I've seen that camp. It was brand new and unfinished. It wasn't being used when I left.'

Gretchen looked at the map too. 'Some SS men came to our school and told us a camp was going to open soon and they'd be looking for people to work in it,' she said.

The two Intelligence officers were very interested in what Tilly and Gretchen had to tell them, and Clara was kept busy translating everything that was said.

'Maybe Hans drew the map,' Tilly said. 'He seemed to be living in the forest next to the camp. But I don't see how he could have put the map in Wuffly's locket – unless he did it when I saw him at Hamburg Station before coming here.'

'When Wuffly ran away!' said Gretchen. 'He could have put it in there then. I always thought it was strange how Wuffly found her way home after she followed your train out of the station. She was somehow sitting in the garden when I woke up.'

'Well, however it got there, this map is very helpful indeed,' one of the officers said.

Talking about Hans made Tilly think of the Golem he'd given to her. It was in her pocket, but she didn't think they would be interested in a little clay figurine or know what he represented. She very much hoped Hans was OK.

'Can we see Wuffly now?' she said to Clara, but Clara shook her head.

'Unfortunately, your dog has run off again and she's lost.'

Chapter 30

The snow had grown even deeper by the time Wuffly woke from her full-up-with-fish nap. Soft whiteness now covered the hollow log she'd been lying inside.

The dachshund shivered with the cold, but at least the log protected her from the wind. She curled up even smaller and closed her eyes again.

'Wuffly! Wuffly!' a voice called in the distance.

The sound came from far away, but the little dog's hearing was four times more acute than a human's. Her ears pricked up. She knew that voice.

'Wu-ffly!'

It was Tilly. *Tilly was calling her!*

Wuffly squeezed out of the hollow log and went racing towards the sound. It was coming from the other side of the frozen pond. Wuffly ran across the ice towards it.

At first the ice held her slight weight.

'*Wuffly!*' Tilly cried with joy when she saw her.

Wuffly ran even faster, her paws slipping and sliding on the ice. She was so focused on Tilly waving just ahead of her that she didn't even see the hole in the ice until she'd fallen through it and disappeared.

Tilly screamed.

The icy water was so, so cold as Wuffly sank down into it. She bobbed up again and struggled to get out, but the hole was small and the ice too slippery to get a grip.

The cold was quickly spreading through her little body, making it hard to struggle, making it hard to fight, making it hard to do anything other than sink below the water and sleep.

'*Wuffly!*' Tilly's terrified voice tore through the winter air. '*Wuffly!*'

Tilly ran to the frozen water's edge.

'No!' Gretchen said, grabbing Tilly's arm before she could venture on to the ice. 'You can't do that!' Every German child knew how dangerous frozen water could be.

Gretchen pulled off her long scarf and Tilly did the same. They tied the two of them together. Tilly held on to one end and Gretchen threw the other end out across the icy lake to Wuffly.

The dog's little head poked out of the hole and grabbed the end of the scarf with her sharp teeth.

The girls pulled and Wuffly's paws scrambled and pushed with every ounce of strength that she had left. Her head came up further and a moment later her little body was out and she was running across the frozen lake to Tilly, her teeth still gripping the scarf.

'Wuffly, Wuffly!' Tilly cried over and over again as the shivering, soaking little dog ran into her arms. Tilly hugged and hugged Wuffly to her.

Tilly and Gretchen had gone on ahead of the Wards, kennel staff and the Army Intelligence men a short time before, but just at that moment, they all came running through the trees.

'We found her!' Gretchen said.

She spoke in German, but Clara didn't bother to translate her words because Gretchen's happy face said it all. Plus Wuffly was there for all to see – safe, but shivering – in Tilly's arms.

They immediately headed back to the kennels, where Tilly was given a blanket to wrap Wuffly in and Clara hurried to make some hot tea for everyone.

'Tilly likes it with lots of sugar,' Mrs Ward called after her as Gretchen ran to help Clara.

'What a pretty little dog,' the kennel maids and trainees said to each other as they went back and forth past the little dachshund wrapped in her warm blanket on Tilly's lap.

Tilly smiled and kissed the top of Wuffly's furry head.

'Now, Wuffly, what else can you tell us?' one of the Army Intelligence officers said, crouching down and looking closely at the little dog. But she didn't have any more clues from Hans on her.

Tilly stroked Wuffly and the man stood up.

'Maybe we'll never know who hid the map in your Wuffly's collar,' he said, 'but I'm very grateful to whoever did.'

Wuffly looked up at Tilly and made happy little crying sounds as she nuzzled her.

'I'm so glad I found you too,' Tilly said, brushing away the tears of happiness that ran down her face. It had been so long since she'd seen Wuffly, she wanted to hold her forever.

Everyone was talking all around them, but for Tilly and her dog, no words were needed. They were just happy to be back together.

'I can't bear to leave Wuffly,' Tilly told Mrs Ward, when she came over to give Wuffly a stroke. Just the thought of being separated again made Tilly feel sick.

'What a sweetie, she is,' Mrs Ward said, and Tilly nodded.

But Wuffly would have to stay at the kennels for six months – it was the law. And after that, all would depend on whether her next foster family would let her have a dog. Poor Wuffly. It was so horribly unfair. Tilly pressed her face into the little dog's fur.

Mrs Bronson touched Tilly on the shoulder and she looked up.

'Mr Ward and I have been talking, and you don't have to go if you don't want to,' Mrs Bronson said, with Clara translating. 'Wuffly can't come with you, but you and your friend Gretchen could stay with her here. We're desperate for extra kennel maids, even trainees, especially now . . . and the Wards have all told me how you want to work with animals and what a wonderful, animal-loving, hard-working addition you would be.'

Tilly could hardly believe her ears. She looked over at the Wards in amazement. They were so kind. 'I do want to work with animals and I will work hard,' she promised.

'Me too?' said Gretchen.

Clara laughed. 'You too! We need all the help we can get.'

'You mean it. You really mean it?' Tilly said as Wuffly looked up at her and wagged her tail.

'But where would we stay?' Gretchen asked.

'In the bungalow where all the kennel maids live, of course,' Clara said. 'There's plenty of room.'

'But what about clothes – I've only got what I'm wearing,' Gretchen told her.

'You'll be given your kennel-maid's uniform,' Mrs Bronson said. 'And you'll be paid – although not much, as you'll have to start off as apprentices. But you'll get more than your food and lodging.'

'And I'd be with Wuffly!' said Tilly.

'And all the other amazing dogs and cats here . . .' said Gretchen.

'And have us kennel maids for friends,' added one of the apprentice girls, who looked about the same age as Tilly and Gretchen.

'We can drop off your suitcase tomorrow,' Mrs Ward told Tilly.

'Dad often comes over here with his work for the RSPCA,' Michael said, 'and we could come with him; it's not that far, so we'd still see you.'

'This'd be the perfect place for picnics once it's warm,' Mrs Ward said.

Tilly smiled. It all sounded wonderful. She imagined her father, Aunt Hedy and Oma here too, enjoying a picnic in the woods. She felt a sudden pang of sadness as she thought of Opa. He would have loved it here as well and so would her mum. She liked to imagine that the two of them were together now.

'So what do you think?' Mrs Bronson asked Tilly and Gretchen. 'Would you like to help out here?'

'We'd love to!' said Tilly and Gretchen together. Wuffly wagged her tail, as Tilly hugged her, because she'd love it most of all.

Six months later, in the early hours of the morning, a small, black-and-tan dachshund, wearing a woven collar of red and gold, slipped off the kennel maid's narrow bed to make her nightly patrol. The bungalow was warm and full of the sounds of people sleeping.

The little dog padded out through the half-open bedroom door and into the kitchen where a mouse lived under the stove. The dachshund's black nose sniffed at the spot where the mouse was hiding, but the tiny creature didn't peep out.

Behind the doors beyond the kitchen, other apprentice kennel maids slept. Wuffly checked on them all, unnoticed, her dark intelligent, inquisitive eyes seeing far more in the dark than any human eyes could. At last she headed back to where she had come from – the small room with two beds squashed inside it and Tilly and Gretchen sleeping in them.

The little dachshund's short legs jumped easily on to the nearest bed. She curled up, but didn't go back to sleep. Wuffly listened and waited, waited for another day with Tilly to begin.

Epilogue

Sharona and her classmates had been less than impressed by the two very old ladies and their dachshund with flecks of grey in her fur when they'd walked into the classroom.

Sharona was a refugee, like several of her fellow pupils. How could these old ladies know what it was like to be hated and persecuted so badly in your own country that you were forced to leave?

Abass rolled his eyes. How could they possibly know what it was like to be a refugee?

'What are they doing here?' Sharona whispered to her friend Meera. Why had the teacher invited them? The smiling elderly ladies were older than Sharona's grandparents, still back in the war zone, older even than her great-grandparents would have been.

The aged dog lay down in the middle of the classroom floor and started to snore.

'We became friends back in Germany on our first day at kindergarten . . .' the old lady with the plait told the children.

'Wuffly wasn't even born then,' the other old lady said with a smile.

The children listened as Tilly and Gretchen told them the story of the *Kindertransport* and how they'd come to England back in 1938.

'. . . And Wuffly lived to be an old, old dog of more than twenty years, with daughters and sons, grandpuppies, great-grandpuppies and even great-great-grandpuppies around her,' Tilly said when they finally ended their talk an hour later.

'Any questions?' Gretchen asked the children.

There were lots.

'Is that Wuffly?' Abass asked, pointing at the dog on the floor.

The old lady with the long black plait that reached so far down her back she could have sat on it, shook her head.

'No, that's Tante – it means "auntie",' Tilly told him. 'Wuffly and Tante never met. But she's Wuffly's great-great-great-great-granddaughter. Tante's named after *Tante* Truus Wijsmuller, a brave Dutch lady who, along with many other brave people, helped thousands of Jewish children to safety. Every time I look at my own furry Tante, I think of her and I am grateful.'

'Other people helped the children too?' Halim asked.

'Oh yes, of course, and most of them aren't remembered at all.'

'The Albanian people rescued and hid thousands of Jews from persecution,' piped up Besjana, who sat next to Sharona. 'We have a code of honour called *besa*. It means "to keep the promise".'

Tilly nodded. 'There were more Jews living in Albania at the end of the Second World War than at the start,' she said. 'Albania succeeded where many other countries failed.'

'What happened to you after the War was over?' asked Meera.

'We stayed in England. It had become our home and we loved working at the kennels,' Gretchen told her.

'But I always knew that one day I wanted to help other refugees in need,' Tilly said.

'And other people who were being persecuted,' said Gretchen.

Tilly nodded. 'Children who'd been part of the *Kindertransport* weren't in contact with each other for many years. We just got on with our new lives as best we could,' she told the class. 'But then we began to meet up and I started talking in schools and at different groups about the *Kindertransport* and what had happened on *Kristallnacht*. I didn't want it to be forgotten.'

'At first it was hard to talk about. Lots of people had buried what had happened to them. They thought if they didn't talk about it they might forget, I suppose,' Gretchen said.

'But you never do forget, do you?' asked Sharona.

Gretchen looked at her intently and then shook her head. 'No, you never do forget,' she said.

The children had so many questions that just about everyone had their hand up.

'What about your families?'

'Aunt Hedy was sent to a female concentration camp, but survived due to her sewing skills. She was made to sew swastika flags for the Nazis. After the War she went to live in Palestine. I never saw the rest of my family again,' Tilly said with a note of sadness.

'My father sent a letter to the Wards' address. It said he was prepared to face the consequences of disobeying orders,' Gretchen told the children. 'Both my mother and father passed away years ago. Fritz went on to become a well-known German Shepherd dog trainer.'

'What happened to Hans?' Meera asked Tilly.

'Did you see him again?' asked someone else.

'What about the *shofar*?'

Tilly shook her head. 'Sadly, I never did see Hans again, but I do know *shofar*s were sounded in celebration throughout the world when the Nazis surrendered in 1945. I like to think of Hans blowing the one he saved. All I have left from the Golem Hans gave me are these little pieces of clay.'

'You broke it!' Adi said. Surely she should have been more careful with something so precious.

Tilly shook her head again. 'No, I didn't break it – I always treasured it. But then one day, many years after it had been given to me, I showed my little Golem to a friend who was a jeweller and . . .'

The children waited as the old ladies grinned at each other and the secret they shared.

'The little pieces of glass that had been used for the eyes and mouth weren't actually glass. They were . . .'

'Diamonds!' the children said as one. Gretchen laughed while nodding her head.

'We were able to help many refugee children with the money from Hans's Golem.' Tilly smiled.

'The Holocaust Remembrance Centre in Israel, Yad Vashem, has a list of people who helped Jewish people during the War,' Gretchen said. 'Those who hid and fed them, helped them to escape, pretended their children were their children. All sorts of things.'

'We should have that today. Awards for people who help refugees. Encourage other people to help them too,' Sharona said, and Abass nodded.

'Maybe we should.'

'The *Stolpersteines* help us to remember as well,' Tilly said.

'*Stolper*– what?' said Abass.

'Little brass stepping stones, memorial plaques, put in the ground outside the homes of the victims of the Nazis. It's said that a person is only forgotten when their name is.'

'Something that bad could never happen again though, could it?' Adi asked.

'Not if we speak out and don't let it,' Gretchen told him.

'We are the hands and feet of those who are not able to make this world a brighter place any longer,' Tilly said.

As the class watched, the elderly dachshund looked up at her and wagged her tail, just like Wuffly used to.

Acknowledgements

The Lost War Dog, more than any of my books so far, has involved meeting and sharing information with many wonderful people. Each encounter and contact has led to another.

My work as a children's author involves lots of school visits and I was delighted with the enthusiastic response from Chantry Academy when the story was little more than an idea.

I knew from the very beginning that this book wouldn't be complete without showing the hard work that current *Kindertransport* survivors do, both by telling their personal stories and as supporters of modern-day refugees.

My good friend Sally Freeman, whose dog Coco sometimes stood in for Wuffly in my imagination, introduced me to a neighbour, Pat Arato, refugee supporter and campaigner.

The Holocaust Educational Trust's aim is to motivate future generations to speak out against intolerance. They kindly allowed me to participate in one of their informative and insightful residential teacher-training weekends. I learnt almost more than I could take in and was fascinated to hear about a *Torah*, stolen from a burning pyre in Hamburg during *Kristallnacht* by fourteen-year-old Isaac Schwartz, who then buried it in his garden, where it remained from 1938 to 2015 when it was dug up. The *Torah* has now been painstakingly restored and displayed.

As well as the wonderful speakers and course leaders, Cat Kirkland and Ben Fuller, I also met Lynda Ford-Horne, who sang a beautiful, haunting Jewish carol and introduced me to the story of Walter Kammerling and his wife, Herta, both *Kindertransport* survivors, who met in the UK as teenagers and married in 1944.

Over the past three years I have been learning British Sign Language, something I now wish I'd done years ago. I've made many new friends within it and I am so grateful to my teacher, Jagjeet Rose, for his continued enthusiasm at each new discovery I made and the new signs I needed to learn for this book. It was so exciting to learn about the deaf children who also came over on the *Kindertransport*, and once I knew of them I was determined to find out more.

Jagjeet told me about Peter Brown, a deaf history lecturer at City Lit in London, who was more than generous with books, his time and knowledge. Peter put me in touch with the Deaf History Association, who told me of the Jewish Deaf Association, who were also more than helpful and welcoming. I was then led to sign language interpreter Gloria Ogborn and her mother, Anne Senchal, who is the last of the deaf *Kindertransport* survivors. I feel very lucky to have found them and grateful for the information and photographs they shared with me.

Anne uses sign language and, fortunately, even with my limited level three ability, we were able to sign-chat, although my main memory of our first meeting is of us laughing together. Anne's story was fascinating and her signed description of her first taste of English tea unforgettably funny!

On a sadder note, Anne, who was previously Anna Marschner, vividly remembered the horror of seeing, as a young girl on the street with her mother, a Nazi soldier shooting a disabled man. She recalled the Hitler Youth boys coming into her residential school playground and attacking the deaf children (she and her brother, Horst, pretended they were not Jewish to escape). She told me how her headmaster was taken away by the *Gestapo* and then returned weeks later with the announcement that a few of the children, including Anna and Horst, were going to England on the *Kindertransport* almost immediately, despite having no papers, along with a non-deaf stowaway.

I am very grateful for all the information, personal stories and experiences shared that brought my own fictional story to life.

On the actual physical book-writing side, my editors Emma Jones and Sara Jafari were continually encouraging and insightful. Working with editors like them makes my work as a children's book writer a delight. ☺

My friend and agent, Clare Pearson, whose valued and considered opinions are always treasured. Thank you also to my wider team at Puffin: my amazing copy editors and proofreaders Mary O'Riordan, Steph Barrett, Pippa Shaw and Pippa Durn, Adam Webling for producing this book, Angelo Rinaldi for illustrating such a wonderful cover and Bella Jones for designing it, Louise Dickie for the brilliant PR work she does, and sales experts Kat Baker and Rozzie Todd.

And finally, my thanks, as always, must go to my family. My dear husband, Eric, whose support makes such a difference, and who often helped with the sometimes overwhelmingly sad research. Thanks also to golden retriever Freya for putting up with a distracted 'mum' and lastly a huge welcome to our newest family addition, puppy Ellie, whose sweet, funny, furry little self brings us utter joy.

Glossary

anti-Semitism: hostile or unfair treatment of Jewish people, just because they are Jewish.

Aryan: originally referring to people from the Aryāvarta parts of India, the word *Aryan* was used by Hitler to describe his ideal of a 'pure German race'. Obsessed with racial purity, he believed pure-blood Aryans were superior to all others and should have pale skin, blue eyes and blonde hair.

concentration camp: a high-security prison used to hold and persecute large numbers of people, such as political enemies or ethnic minorities and others. Concentration camps became associated with the Nazis during the Second World War.

Fuhlsbüttel (KolaFu): an area of northern Hamburg, in Germany, and the site of a notorious Nazi concentration camp, known as KolaFu. During the Second World War, the camp quickly gained a reputation for horrific suffering and death.

Führer: the German word for 'leader', and the title used by Adolf Hitler to define his absolute authority within Germany's Third Reich from 1933–1945.

Gestapo: the *Geheime Staatspolizei*, or secret police of Nazi Germany, founded by Hermann Göring in 1933.

Grynszpan, Herschel Feibel (28 March 1921–8 May 1945): born in Germany to Polish-Jewish parents, Grynszpan was responsible for the murder of a German diplomat, Ernst vom Rath, on 7 November 1938 in Paris. He told police the killing was to avenge 12,000 persecuted Jews. The Nazis used the assassination as an excuse for launching *Kristallnacht*, their campaign of organized violence against Jews throughout Germany.

Hitler, Adolf (20 April 1889–30 April 1945): born in Austria, Hitler rose to power in Germany as a politician and mesmerizing public speaker, becoming leader of the Nazi Party in 1921, and chancellor of the Third Reich in 1933. Having crushed all opposition, Hitler set about transforming Germany into his vision of a 'pure Aryan race', and blaming the country's problems on the Jews and other minorities. In 1938, he began a campaign of territorial expansion when his armies marched into Austria and Czechoslovakia. Then on 1 September 1939, Hitler's forces invaded Poland, which led to the outbreak of the Second World War. In April 1945, he committed suicide in his underground bunker in Berlin to avoid capture when it became obvious that Germany had been defeated.

Hitler Youth: known as *Hitlerjugend* in German, this was the young boys' section of the Nazi Party in Germany, set up by Hitler in 1933 to instruct members in Nazi ideology. By 1936, all young 'Aryan' German boys were expected to join, having first been investigated to make sure they had no Jewish relatives. Two leagues also existed for girls. The *Jungmädel*, or Young Girls' League, was for those aged ten to fourteen, then the *Bund Deutscher Mädel*, or League of German Girls, took those aged fourteen to eighteen. The girls were trained for comradeship, household duties and motherhood.

Kindertransport: an organized rescue mission that enabled thousands of mainly Jewish children from Nazi Germany and Nazi-occupied Austria, Czechoslovakia and Poland to escape persecution and be transported to safety in England via the

Netherlands. The first *Kindertransport* left Berlin by train on 1 December 1938, then crossed the English Channel by boat, arriving in Harwich on 2 December. In the following nine months, almost 10,000 mostly Jewish children travelled to England on the *Kindertransport*s, and they were often the only members of their families to survive the Second World War.

Kristallnacht (9–10 November 1938): known as 'The Night of Broken Glass', or the 'November Pogrom', this was a campaign of organized violence by the Nazis, aimed at Jews and their property across Germany. In two days, over 250 synagogues were burned, 7,000 Jewish businesses destroyed, at least ninety-one Jewish people were killed and Jewish cemeteries, hospitals, schools and houses were vandalized and left in ruins while the emergency services stood by and watched. The morning after the pogrom, 30,000 German Jewish men were arrested for the crime of being Jewish, and sent to concentration camps.

Nazi Party: the National Socialist German Workers' Party, known as the Nazi Party, was a far-right political group in Germany, active between 1920 and 1945. They aimed to create an 'Aryan master race', by exterminating all those they considered inferior, such as political opponents, the mentally or physically disabled, and 'foreign' races, especially Jews. The Nazis planned the 'Final Solution' – genocide on a massive scale that resulted in the murder of 6,000,000 Jews and millions of other victims, in what has become known as the Holocaust.

Neuengamme: established in December 1938 by the SS in a suburb of Hamburg, northern Germany, this was a branch of Sachsenhausen concentration camp. It was located in the grounds of an abandoned brickworks on a tributary of the River Elbe. When the camp was finally liberated by British soldiers on 2 May 1945, nearly 43,000 people had already died there from hunger, disease, exhaustion or violence. The grounds are now open to the public and serve as a memorial and research centre.

pogrom: an organized, violent and destructive riot aimed at an ethnic or religious group, particularly the Jews.

***Polenaktion* (28 October 1938):** the German word for 'Polish action', used to describe the arrest and forcible expulsion across the border to Poland of many thousands of Polish Jews who had been living in Nazi Germany.

rabies: a serious viral infection of the brain and nerves that can be transmitted to humans through the bite or scratch of an infected animal. Dogs are the main source of rabies.

SA, the: founded in 1921 by Hitler, the *Sturmabteilung*, or Storm Detachment, was the Nazi Party's original paramilitary wing. The Storm Troopers played an important role in Hitler's rise to power in the 1920s and 1930s. They were also known as Brownshirts from the colour of their uniforms.

Sachsenhausen: a Nazi concentration camp at Oranienburg, north of Berlin, Germany, from 1936 to the end of the Third Reich in May 1945. The camp held political prisoners, as well as Jews (including Herschel Grynszpan), Roma, homosexuals, Jehovah's Witnesses and others. The prisoners were treated with great cruelty, scarcely fed and openly murdered. Today, Sachsenhausen is open to the public as a memorial to the victims.

shofar: an ancient musical instrument made out of a ram's horn, the shofar is blown like a bugle and used during Jewish religious services.

SS, the: founded in 1925, the *Schutzstaffel*, or Protection Squadrons, originally served as Hitler's bodyguards, but later became one of the most powerful and feared organizations in all of Nazi Germany. After proving they had no Jewish ancestry, recruits recieved military training, during which they were taught that they were the elite – not only of the Nazi party, but of all humankind.

Stolperstein: literally meaning 'stumbling stone', a *Stolperstein* is a small concrete cube with a brass plate on top, inscribed with the name and dates of victims of Nazi persecution. These memorials can be found set into pavements outside the last-known houses or workplaces of those commemorated. The *Stolpersteine* Art Project was initiated by German artist Gunter Demnig in the 1990s. Today, the *Stolpersteine* Art Project is part of a research project into what life was like for such minorities during the Nazi era.

synagogue: a Jewish house of worship.

Third Reich: the name given to the German state between 1933 and 1945 when Adolf Hitler and the Nazi Party transformed the country into a dictatorship, controlling all aspects of life.

Wijsmuller, Truus (21 April 1896–30 August 1978): Geertruida Wijsmuller-Meijer, known as

Truus, was a member of the Dutch resistance during the Second World War. She played a very important part in organizing and guiding the *Kindertransport*s, enabling many Jewish children to escape persecution in Germany and other European countries, and travel to a safer life in England.

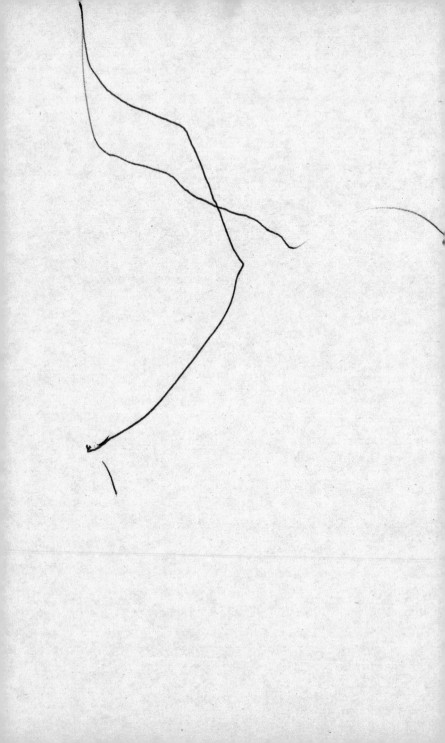